THE REUNION

ILIRIANA RAMA

Contents

For the Heroic Women of Kosovo
whose resilience and courage is an endless source of inspiration,

and

For my parents, whose love resides within me, guiding my soul.

"One day you will press to your bosom
The fallen leaves of your seasons
And will search for yourself in vain
On the forgotten pathways of a generation."

From a poem "Before Elegy"
    by Azem Shkreli

Map of Kosovo and Surrounding Area of the Balkans

ONE

BESA

Looking through the airplane window, she strugled to recognize the landscape of her home country, which she hadn't seen for twenty years.

The mountains and valleys felt familiar, as did the small houses' new red roofs, a sign of their reconstruction after the war. Roads wound up and down the hills traversing fields of wheat, stretching across vast plains.

It was a beautiful sunny morning in June. She felt both restless and tired from the long trip. She eagerly awaited for the plane to land, having been unable to sleep during the long flight from New York to Vienna. The shorter trip from Vienna to Prishtina was equally trying due to excitement, mixed emotions, and anticipation.

As the plane neared its destination, she reflected on the passage of time and how short and long her life seemed at the same time, and she felt both older and younger than her forty years. So many things had happened to her and so many changes and upheavals took place during her life that she felt like she had lived more than her forty years.

The twenty-year absence from her country had flown by in so many ways and dragged on and on in others. Living two distinct lives in two very different countries had shaped her into two personas prompting her to ponder the concept of self evolution. She remembered having read somewhere that the cells in one's body regenerate and replace themselves every seven years, which made her believe that people change whether they realise it or not, whether they get uprooted from their countries or not. She acknowledged a significant change within herself especially from the last time she was here, in the city where she was born. Her transformation extended beyond mere ageing and passing of time. It was more due to the impact of living in a different social environment from the one that she was born in, from speaking in a different language than the one she grew up speaking and embracing a different worldview that living in a place as diverse as New York would bring onto a person.

For two decades, she had regarded New York as home, even if she thought about her country of birth everyday. New York was a big part of who she had become.

Twenty years is such a long time, she thought, not knowing what to expect from her decision to move back. She often thought: What if she had never left this country? How would her life look like now? What kind of a person would she be?

The more she wondered and asked herself these questions, the more she was inclined to believe in destiny beyond one's control that determined people's lives, sometimes against their wishes or plans. It wasn't her choice to leave Kosova or to live through the horrors that she had experienced, so it must have been destiny, she concluded.

Also, the decision to return home wasn't hers alone but it

stemmed partly from new circumstances in her workplace and again she couldn't shake the feeling that fate was responsible for this too.

The workings of fate and destiny were on her mind too, the morning that her boss had asked her in the office for the exciting news: "The US embassy in Prishtina requires an employee fluent in local language and customs and with US education to provide a balanced perspective. I immediately thought of you and I believe you're the perfect fit" her boss had explained excitedly. She was shocked at this unbelievable opportunity coming at her. She didn't know what to say beyond Thank you and thinking all the time about the mysterious ways in which destiny must have worked its way through this. It was meant for her to return home after twenty years, she thought. It was also the right time.

She was good at her job as an assistant to the director of the organisation that dealt with Foreign Affairs, a dream job that she had landed after studying vigorously at NYU for years. She graduated with honours in Political Science and worked hard to get to the position that she had, but she hadn't anticipated that an offer to work in her home country was even possible.

Despite her professional achievements, she had felt a void in her personal life that she didn't know how to fill. Her successful career driven by workaholic tendencies and perfectionism couldn't make up for this void that she felt especially since her divorce from James, five years ago. The prospect of returning home, even though exciting and long awaited, filled her with anxiety. She feared another complete fresh start in her life, another big decision of moving to another country, even if it was the one where she was born and had lived in for the first 19 years of her life. She wasn't looking forward to the part where her mind would go back in time and deal with the past that she had avoided thinking about as much as possible.

She wondered if the time was right to reflect on the past in order to move forward with her life. To some people, this way of thinking might not make sense and they would avoid looking backward at their life. It would seem absurd especially to James who had constantly urged her to not look back, to leave the past behind. The anticipation of returning home had been a long-awaited mix of excitement and apprehension, lingering for far too long. Now she felt like she was about to complete a full circle of her life.

"Where are you from?" the young woman sitting next to her with her baby in her lap had asked her earlier. Besa paused for a moment and then replied "I'm from Prishtina." "Have you been away on holiday?" she asked again, trying to make small talk while gently rocking her crying baby in her arms. Once more, Besa paused. She smiled politely at the young woman. She disliked these types of questions; they seemed simple, but they were anything but.

At this particular point in her life, Besa found herself uncertain of how to answer that question and what it truly meant to be from somewhere. Was it determined by birthplace? Was it where she had spent the majority of her adult years? Was it where her ancestors lay buried? Truthfully, Besa struggled with how to address this question. In the United States such questions were seldom posed, largely because everyone hailed from diverse backgrounds. How could she convey to this young woman that it has become hard for her to answer that question because in America, individuals reinvented themselves daily. They embraced the freedom to sculpt their identities, to alter their paths, to adopt new personas, and to relocate without feeling tied to familial obligations. For most of them, they were simply Americans, irrespective of their origins. Initially perplexing, Besa eventually got used to this concept and even found it emancipating. It made her feel guilty at times thinking about allowing herself such boundless freedom, to be who you wanted - something that would be viewed as self-centred, unconventional and even selfish in Kosovo back at the time when she was young. Above all, she was raised by her parents with the understanding that individuality or separate existence shouldn't be her primary focus. She was ingrained with the belief that she was part of something greater than herself - a member of the esteemed Kelmendi family, with a storied history dating back to ancient times. It was up to each member of the family, including herself, to uphold the honour of her ancestors and preserve their legacy. Additionally, she belonged to a broader community, the Albanians, who had long endured second class status in Yugoslavia. From her upbringing, she internalised the notion that her individual actions, whether good or bad, virtuous or otherwise, would reflect upon the reputation and standing of her nation as a whole. This mindset, instilled by her parents, emphasised the interconnectedness of her identity with her family, community, and nation, discouraging her from viewing herself as a solitary individual detached from these collective identities.

If anyone in the US inquired about her origins, she proudly declared herself from Kosovo. With a sparkle in her eyes, she would proceed to elaborate on the exact location of Kosovo, stating it as the youngest country in the world - a Newborn, just like the renowned monument erected after the war in the capital Prishtina proclaimed. She remembered watching on her television set in the US when that monument was unveiled on the day of Kosovo's Independence, enveloped in a sea of celebrants. She had watched in awe with tears of joy streaming down her face. The simplicity of the monument, composed solely of enormous letters spelling out the word "NEWBORN" in vibrant yellow, radiated a striking sincerity and directness in its message. The monument had a childlike innocence and joy in itself, she thought and it reminded her of Manhattan's iconic LOVE monument. Yet, unlike its counterpart, the Newborn monument bore the weight of profound pain. It made her emotional as she felt that it stood as a testament to the countless innocent lives lost, the rivers of blood spilled, and the sacrifices made upon which this country was founded. For many generations, freedom and independence had been a cherished dream and the realisation came at a staggering cost - akin to the agony of childbirth.

Besa glanced at the young mother sitting next to her in the cramped plane and offered a smile. "I've been visiting some friends," she said, avoiding eye contact. "Now, I'm returning home." she said smiling. She turned back to the window thinking about the words that she just said, pondering the truth behind them. She didn't know why she lied to the young woman. Did she truly feel like these past twenty years were just a fleeting visit to another country? Was she ready to resume life here as if nothing had changed? She wasn't sure what the answer to these questions was but what mattered most was the nearing destination. Almost there. Home.

Stepping out of the plane, emotions engulfed her. Her heart trembled as she tried to hold back tears. Tears weren't her usual way of dealing with emotions, but today she felt like a bottle of soda fizzing and about to burst in the midst of the crowd. She bit her lip, dabbing her nose and eyes with a paper napkin, struggling to keep composed. The large banners proclaiming "Welcome Home Compatriots" above the customs gates only heightened her emotions.

As the courteous officer checked her American passport and noticed her distinctly Albanian name, he warmly greeted her with a "Welcome Home". It took all her strength not to break into loud sobs; instead she nodded and forced a smile through her tears. With her passport stamped, she headed towards the exit, hiding her tired, teary eyes behind dark sunglasses. Would she meet someone she knew from twenty years ago? A neighbour? A school friend perhaps or a distant cousin? Would anyone recognise her after all this time? she wondered. She kind of hoped she would find a familiar face right away, right there at the airport but even if she did and someone would recognize her from the past, who would they see? Would they see the young teenager still residing somewhere deep in her but that she herself couldn't see anymore? Would someone care to find out why and how she changed from a confident, happy teen to a lonely, anxious adult?

The loneliness unique to immigrants in sprawling cities like New York had drained her. It would take time to adjust to conversations and socialising again. Simple chit-chat taken for granted here, would require considerable effort after years of speaking a few basic words a day to anyone in the US.

Besa was a beautiful woman that usually stood out in a crowd especially because of her thick, naturally wavy golden blond hair cascading gracefully to her shoulders. Tall and preferring heels for posture, her slender figure remained unchanged over the years, as she never experienced pregnancy. Despite her captivating appearance, her large, brown eyes concealed a lingering sadness, even when she smiled. She seldom raised her voice, maintaining a quiet demeanour that sometimes felt like a struggle to articulate. Days could pass with scarcely a word spoken. Some mistook her silence for weakness, shyness, or perhaps naivety. Though she acknowledged these traits within herself, with age, she no longer felt defined by them, even though she still kept to herself. Despite her polite and pleasant nature, forming friendships didn't come easily. Opening up to others took time, often leading her to be perceived as cold and reserved. Since her divorce from James she became even less interested in getting to know people or in having intimate conversations with anyone. Yet her mind buzzed incessantly with thoughts and words in the various languages she spoke. She mostly lived inside her head. Immersing herself in work became her refuge; she was always the first to arrive and the last to leave the office. Her job, which she excelled at, brought her satisfaction. There was no need to prove herself anymore; she commanded respect and good will from everyone at the office. Despite this, she maintained a comfortable distance, not making any close friendships. And she preferred it that way.

She scanned the bustling airport, searching once more for a familiar face among the airport youthful workers. They belonged to a different generation, one she couldn't possibly have known. She couldn't wait to see her mother and run into her arms. Exhaustion, excitement, happiness, and sadness intertwined within her, creating a whirlwind of emotions.

Stepping out of the airport building, she was met with a sea of people eagerly awaiting their loved ones. Anxiety surged as she met the intense gazes of strangers waiting for people to come out the door. She squinted trying to pick out the faces of her mother and aunt. She pushed her airport cart forward through the crowd and she heard her name: "Besa, Besa " her aunt called out, manoeuvring her way towards her. Besa abandoned her cart and embraced her. Though younger than her mother, her aunt appeared noticeably aged since their last meeting. Despite their regular phone calls and exchanged photos, Besa hadn't anticipated this change. "Let's go!", her aunt exclaimed, "Shpresa is waiting for us in the car. She couldn't contain her emotions and decided to wait there." Taking the cart, she helped Besa to navigate through the crowd toward the parking lot. Besa's mother emerged from the car, tears streaming down her face, as she reached out to embrace her. Despite her tears, a broad smile adorned her pale, fragile face. "Finally!" , she exclaimed, "Finally, my sweetheart, you're home. This is the happiest day of my life."

She had missed her mother so much; the comforting embrace, the gentle scent of lavender shampoo in her hair, and the radiant smile that rivalled the warmth of Spring sunshine. Just like the essence of her name Shpresa - "Hope", her mother had always been a beacon of hope, a reassurance that all was well in the world, and that everything would turn out to be alright, no matter the circumstances.

The journey from the airport to her parents' modest apartment in the heart of Prishtina lasted about 30 minutes. As she glanced out the window, she struggled to recognise the bustling streets, the unfamiliar highway, and even her own neighbourhood. Everything seemed so different.

———

March 1999

Boom...boom...boom...

A loud bang came from the downstairs entrance door of the apartment building. The loud thuds that sounded like thunder, jolted her awake. She opened her eyes into the darkness of her small room and held her breath. She remained as still as possible hoping that the noise would go away. But it didn't.

It took Besa a few moments to figure out what the noises were and where they were coming from. She tried to ease her breath as she listened. The clamour was getting louder. She heard thudding up the stairs of the building and the loud knocks seemed to be moving closer and closer to their apartment door. In the silence between the thunderous blows, she could hear screams, the cries of children, and the splintering of doors being broken into. It felt like the entire building was trembling, and that the peace of the night had been torn like a threadbare cloth.

Besa's heart pounded against her chest with growing intensity as the clamouring drew ever closer to the threshold of their apartment door. The banging was going on and on without stopping, and became louder and louder with every passing minute. She heard loud sharp commands being given, shouted in a menacing manner. Trepidation filled her as she realised this was the cacophony of a mob of villains ready to slaughter everyone in their sight.

Besa now knew exactly what was happening although she wasn't sure whether everything was real or just a figment of her nightmare. This was the horrid reality of war unfolding before her. The Serbian police and paramilitary forces were swarming up the stairs of the apartment buildings all over the city, pounding on each door and summoning the residents out. They were being sent away from their homes and neighbourhoods, away from their city and their country. What would happen to her and her parents? Where would they go? What would become of them? It was chilly and dark in that early spring morning. Her heart sank with the fear of the unknown. How could these people be so heartless and callous? Why couldn't they just let them be? Her room was pitch black and she thought she had gone blind for a second. The only movement in her dark room was the rapid beating of her heart. Was it morning yet? She could not tell as she started to feel dizzy, and a sense of weakness started crawling through her joints like a snake.

She must have been asleep for at least a couple of hours as her body sometimes just shut off from the constant tension that she felt. The loud noise of these new unsettling sounds felt like an interruption from the now familiar whizzing of falling bombs, machine gun fire and air raid sirens that had been ringing through the city day and night for the past few days. Naturally, the war had made sleeping impossible but, up to now, the war had felt as an absurdity that was somehow distant from the city. Well, now the war was certainly upon them, coming to their front door. Her heart thumped against her chest and its noise was making her ears ring. Her breathing got quicker as she felt she couldn't get enough air and thought she was going to suffocate. Each successive thump against the apartment door got entwined with her heartbeat.

She had secretly watched those soldiers from time to time through her bedroom window during the past few days since she and her parents had basically locked themselves indoors. She had watched them secretly by carefully drawing back the corner of the blanket that her mother had pinned to the window. The fear from those soldiers drifted quietly around their home and in their neighbourhood. It hung like an invisible water current, ready to overtake them and swallow them to death. Although she and her parents never talked about fear, she could feel it in her bones. She felt like this fear was disregarded in the same way as a heavy smoker disregards the cancer warnings. Although they could clearly see what the soldiers and paramilitaries were doing, they still hoped that the horrors would somehow bypass their home, as crazy as that hope seemed.

The blanket on her window was supposed to shield and protect her both from the soldier's attention, and from the danger of shattered glass should a bullet or a bomb come flying through the window. It was an old blanket decorated in large flowery patterns of varying shades of brown that had belonged to her grandmother. Now that those soldiers were marching up their apartment building, eliciting screams and tears of terrified people, that same blanket had somehow become a reminder of their naïve underestimation of those soldiers' capability to dismantle their innocent and feeble attempts to be vigilant and resilient in these frightful moments. Besa's mother had secured the blanket with nails to the four corners of the window, when Nato began airstrikes against the Serbian forces with the intention of ending a brutal war against innocent people just like her and her family. Besa and her parents had been hopeful the day that bombing started. They thought they would finally get to see the end of this horrible war and maybe even be able to go back to their normal everyday lives soon.

"Milošević must be stopped now" President Clinton had said.

She had heard the news with her own ears the night before the air strikes began, in a small radio with a broken antenna, that they listened to every night, keeping the volume as low as possible, close to their ears. Since then, every morning, they hoped that that would be the last day of war. But it still went on.

Now the soldiers were knocking on their door and Besa felt that she and her parents wouldn't be saved after all. This moment of dread felt like judgement day.

The thick blanket did not let any light through into her room, yet she looked in the direction of the window anyway. Her only hope of escape would require her to move to the window and then take a leap of faith while climbing down the drain pipe from the fourth floor of the building but she couldn't move, her body seemed rooted to the bed and she was overcome by terror. She felt entangled between a dream and a weird, dark, surreality. She lay in her bed consumed by a potent mixture of fear, rage and regret.

How could she have been so foolish and decided to sleep in her room alone tonight, instead of sleeping in her parents' bedroom like she had done for days now. They had all slept with their clothes on, ready to flee at a moment's notice. They were reminded of the fragility of their existence every night and each passing moment. For days, she and her parents had lived in a state of constant vigilance, their nerves frayed to a breaking point.

But on that night, she let her guard down;in a fleeting moment of defiance,she wanted to feel like a defiant rebel instead of a mere victim of her circumstances. She washed her hair with a bottle of cold water, potted during short periods of time they had meagre rations of running water. She had lathered her hair with lavender-scented shampoo, relishing in the small luxury that this simple act afforded her. In a further act of rebellion, she rummaged through the deep corners of her closet to retrieve a cherished relic of her childhood - a pink nightgown adorned with the likeness of Sleeping

Beauty. Even though it no longer fit her properly, she wore it with a sense of defiant pride, refusing to allow the war to rob her of the comfort of her cherished childhood memories, even if just for a night. This was her way of fighting back against those soldiers that sought to break her spirit and make her feel like a helpless prey hiding in the dark.

However, at this particular moment, she didn't feel brave; the pink nightgown appeared entirely out of place. What was she thinking? She was 19 years old for god's sake. Why did she feel the need to put on a small, ill fitting, pink nightgown with the faded face of the Sleeping Beauty on it? The sense of defiance disappeared giving way to a growing sense of fear and vulnerability. She felt like a little child. She wished she was a little child. Maybe, she thought "they" would have spared her if she was smaller, if she was just a child. Her body didn't match the child that she was inside. The boundaries that had offered her a modicum of safety these past few days were now dissolving before her eyes, leaving her exposed to this relentless onslaught of the outside world. Walls and doors that had seemed somewhat secure,now offered no protection, and even the comfort of her blanket and nightgown seemed to be slipping away.

She closed her eyes tightly and for a fleeting moment she wondered if it were possible to escape her physical body, to leave behind her mortal form and find sanctuary in some other realm. Yet, she didn't have any idea of how one could escape from their physical body or where would one go further than home to feel safe? There was no such place. Nowhere! She thought. There was nowhere to escape.

She heard the front door being forced open. Her parent's voices rose in a frantic Serbian as they tried to reason with the soldiers. She recognised the sound of the stomping boots and the jarring clink of the soldiers' guns. As she stood frozen in fear, Besa's heart sank as she caught a whiff of a thick and suffocating smell seeping through the door. She gasped for air as it occurred to her that she had never thought or imagined how those soldiers smelled. It was always their menacing appearance, their weapons, and their barking commands that had frightened her. But now, she felt like a stench of death was clawing its way down her throat, invading her senses! The horrors that lay beyond her door felt imminent. She smelled death.

The door to her small bedroom flew open with a deafening crash!Two soldiers entered her room. Their silhouettes loomed in the doorway, against the pitch darkness of the room as she absurdly, for a split second, thought about how there had never been any strangers in her bedroom before and how tragic that these were the strangest visitors she could have imagined. The weight of their presence was suffocating. She not only felt frightened but embarrassed somehow. Like she shouldn't have been caught off guard, sleeping like that. Like somehow it was her fault for all of this.

Her body went numb in a sea of fear and her soul trembled as if it sought to escape from the impending horror. The soldiers pointed their guns at her as she stood frozen under her blanket. She stared down the barrels of those guns as if curious if they were real and for a split second, for a brief moment,she became indifferent. Her fear seemed to go away leaving space to some weird feeling of indifference.

An intense heat seemed to emanate from the metal on the tip of the guns and it felt as if it was burning holes in her body.

She wondered how death felt for the person that it happened to, and her mind quickly went on to imagining her own mortality. Would her passing be as peaceful as the lifeless figures that she had seen in the movies? Would she feel pain as her soul departed from her body? Surely, something as quiet and indifferent as death, shouldn't be painful, she thought.

Death was probably just a sunken feeling, a quiet, cold sensation just like the one she was experiencing in those moments. She could hear her mother's soft wailing echoing in the background. Her mournful sobs entered her ears like a sharp blade seeping into the very core of her being, piercing her heart. She felt a deep longing to offer comfort to her mother, to embrace her and to tell her not to worry, that everything would be fine. She couldn't bear to see and hear her mother's grief.

This situation seemed so absurd that in that moment she realised how nothing made sense anymore. At first, there was no urge to scream for help as she realised that no one could help her. She couldn't force herself to make any sound as it seemed that her own voice had been stolen away, leaving her mute and helpless.

A silent plea reverberated through the depths of her soul. She attempted to scream:

Ahhhhhh..... No sound. Only pain. That endless pit of deep, incurable pain.

She was torn between nightmare and reality, between the darkness of the room and fiery light coming from the soldier's silhouettes threatening to engulf her.

Ahhhhh..... She tried to scream again to no avail. Her voice was lost, and it seemed as if she ceased to exist.

————

June, 2019

Besa woke up abruptly from another nightmare, her body was all sweaty and her mind confused. She lay there, in the grip of her nightmare, her heart pounding in her chest, her breaths coming in ragged gasps. The nightmare refused to release her. She opened and closed her eyes forcefully several times and, for a brief moment, she forgot where she was. She forgot that she was home, in the small apartment in the city of Prishtina, the place where she was born and where she had spent her childhood years. As she struggled against the dark with twisted images that plagued her soul, she realised that she was in the very room where her nightmare happened and the fact that she was in that room right now made her feel more confused than usual. She was on the same bed, in the same room with the same walls and same window, and she felt the same sense of unease that she had felt twenty years ago in this place.

She took deep breaths as she tried to calm herself down.

She let her eyes wander around the room, adjusting to the faint light of dawn coming through the window. The door to the room was left slightly open this time as she couldn't sleep in a room with a closed door or without a night light left on since that night, twenty years ago.

She looked around the familiar room as if to make sure that she was really here --the walls were still painted a faint yellow, with shelves holding a collection of books and trinkets—faint nostalgia was giving way to more subtle memories in this room.

She tried to take away her attention from the nightmare and remember the times of joy she had experienced within these four walls and focus on them. It was as though time had stood still in her parent's apartment, frozen in a bygone era. The walls were still adorned with the same old floral wallpaper, the flowy curtains swaying gently, and the furniture that once gleamed with pride was now old and worn out. How could everything remain so unchanged, yet so different? Everything looked smaller to her; her bed,once comfortable, was now tiny and strange. She sighed and closed her eyes, allowing herself to be enveloped in the flood of memories that reminded her how important this room was for her. She could almost hear her friend's joyful laughter, friends that had once filled the room with energy. The images of the countless hours spent in this room, poring over textbooks with her friends, their attention waning constantly as they delved into the world of fantasy and fun instead of school work, came to her mind. The room had seen them through both the highs and lows of their teenage years, a haven of sorts where they could be their truest selves without fear. The memories of her friends' faces and their lively dance parties and impromptu karaoke sessions, trying to impersonate Madonna or the latest dances from Michael Jackson videos came to her mind, bringing a smile to her lips. They had kept themselves entertained for hours on end and had revelled in their youth, their spirits unbridled and free as they pranced around the room, lost in the moment. This room was more than just four walls and a ceiling. It was a symbol of their friendship, a place where they had shared their dreams, hopes and fears. It was a sanctuary where they had grown up together, living in their own world, a testament to the bond that they had shared all those years ago. This room also became a scene of her horrible nightmare too that she wished she could forget.

She glanced at books lined on the shelves on the showcase cabinet. She recognized the brown colour with gold letters book covers of Ismail Kadare books that were a testament to the struggles of Albanian life during the dictatorship in Albania. She had been intimidated by those books, never feeling smart enough to understand them. She had reread them repeatedly during High School Years. Albania had been an enigma for the Albanians in Kosovo and especially her generation. The country was this enigmatic motherland that no one really knew much about and of which they couldn't speak about in Yugoslavia. She tried to get cues from the books and from occasional TV or radio programmes secretly bootlegged by her father when they went to visit her uncle and other relatives in the countryside. Everyone would gather around a small TV to watch in amazement the beautiful folk concerts with an astounding array of national costumes, with songs from every region where Albanians lived regardless of the country they were left out of during the changes of time, they watched the movies spoken in an amazing fluent, standard Albanian accent that she had strived to emulate without success.

The news on the one existing channel of the Communist Albania, showed nothing but the success of the workers and cooperatives in agriculture. She and her family had watched in amazement the beautiful mountains turned into terraces where crops grew by hard working, always smiling people and then they watched as those same workers gathered in the small village cultural centres for artistic events. Everything seemed so perfect and everyone seemed so happy on the Albanian TV channel. An ultimate utopia that they in Kosova had watched secretly in awe. Little did they know about what most of those people paraded on TV screens went through under one of the most isolated dictatorships in the world. Still she remembered her father watching with teary eyes the scenery of Albania, the flag, the songs and the dances. The love for the motherland was sacred, non negotiable!. It was a constant reminder that Albanians in Kosovo were unjustly separated from Albania.

Next to Ismail Kadare's books were the green and white coloured covered books by Fan Noli, and in them were her favourite poems that she had memorised as a child. She still remembered the insides of each of those books and they felt like they were old friends who had waited for her quietly in this room until she returned home after all these years.

The small souvenirs gathered from her parents' travels lined up neatly on the shelves, each with its own story. A wooden sailboat, a reminder of the days spent in Ulqin, Montenegro, with its soft sand and vast sea. The grandiose figure of Scanderbeg, protector of the Albanian people, watched over Besa's beloved family photos, souvenirs, and memories. It looked as if he stood guard with a fierce expression on his face, his beard perfectly groomed, and his famous helmet adorned with a goat's head and horns on his head. Pride radiated from the legendary figure as his eyes swept his domain with vigilant watchfulness.

A small collection of charming porcelain ballerinas brought by her mother from Poland during one of her school trips as a teacher of history, beckoned beside the gallant protector. The matryoshka doll set sat quietly in the corner of the shelf. Besa couldn't quite remember where it had come from - whether it was a gift from a family member who had travelled to Russia. She had been fascinated by those dolls, the way they nested perfectly inside each other. She had spent countless hours making her friends guess how many dolls there were in total, first opening the largest one and revealing the smaller ones inside, to the total astonishment of her friends. It was a game that never got old, a source of endless wonder and intrigue.

A collection of framed photographs was kept on the shelves, each with a unique story and sentiment. From the serious countenance on the black and white engagement photo of her parents to the cheerful memories captured in the photos taken in the garden of her grandparent's home, these cherished images cast a warmth over the room. Besa smiled to herself as she was reminded of the love and closeness of her extended family during her childhood. She fondly recalled spending most of her school summer breaks in the picturesque little village where her father was born and where her grandparents and uncles lived.

She realised how much she had missed everything about home - the familiar sights, the comforting smells she had grown up with and even this small room that she still visited regularly in her nightmares.

She lay there, still paralyzed in fear, her body drenched in sweat as the haunting nightmare lingered in her mind. Taking a deep breath, she rose from the bed and walked towards the window. There was no heavy blanket nailed on its frame now. She opened the window to let a cool morning breeze seep into the room caressing her face, easing the pain that had haunted her through the night. As the dawn broke and the first rays of light crept through the window, she finally felt relieved from the shackles of fear. With each deep breath, she regained her composure, gathering her strength. She was finally home and had come back after twenty years in search of closure, to put an end to the recurring nightmare that had tormented her all these years. But as she stood there still trembling, she wasn't sure if she would ever be totally free of its grip. She had hoped that by coming here, she would find solace in the fact that things had changed, that the country had been liberated, that the war was over and that the police and military of the war were no longer here. But she realised that the reality was far more complex than she had imagined.

As she looked at the city she loved through the window of her childhood room, she could see that the scars of war were still visible in her familiar yet different neighbourhood, in which wounds and trauma still felt raw. She could feel the city's lingering sadness in the air. The sky was somehow hanging low, and people carried it like a burden on their shoulders. The sadness was subtle, of the kind that only a place which had experienced war might bear and that only people who had lived through that war could recognize it.

It was quiet as the sun was slowly lightening up the edges of the mountains surrounding the city. A few cars were already moving on the streets taking people somewhere. A sense of nostalgia that she had felt ever since she came back here two days ago, overtook her once more. Her eyes filled up with tears again for the hundredth time.

She continued looking at the familiar streets, other balconies and windows, in and around the apartment building where she grew up and as the rays of morning sun were filling them with light, she wondered what were the actual feelings of the people that continued to call this place home and came back after they were made to leave on that early March morning of '99. Perhaps the prevailing sadness was only within her. Maybe, despite the tumultuous past, the city now teemed with hope, filled with young people who had grown up in freedom and didn't want to be associated with war and violence. Her own generation, survivors of past horrors, sought closure much like herself. They were determined to build a better future for their children, she could see that. She wondered if she possessed the strength to stay and live here for the rest of her life and fight alongside them. Instead of dwelling in regret and sadness, could she join them in bearing witness to the truth, ensuring that atrocities that had been committed in her country were never forgotten? She had promised herself twenty years ago that she would work tirelessly for the rest of her life, no matter where she lived, to honour the memory of everyone who suffered and perished, including herself and her family and to ensure that such horrors would never be repeated.

With a deep sigh she lifted her arms, stretching them as far as they would go hoping to banish the palpable sense of unease that lingered within her.

"It will pass" - she whispered to herself and with each passing moment, the fear gradually dissipated, replaced by a sense of calm.

She went back to bed and her mind began to race once more with anticipation at the thought of the day that was in front of her and that promised to be full of excitement. The long-awaited Reunion Party with her high school friends was happening that night. The mere thought of seeing her friends' faces after all these years sent a wave of excitement coursing through her veins. Memories of old times and youthful exuberance flooded her mind, bringing a smile to her lips. Over the years she had managed to stay connected with some of her friends through the wonders of social media. She relished the moments when she caught glimpses of their lives through their posts, feeling a sense of joy in the knowledge that they were still connected, after all these years. She thought about their teenage excitement and anticipation of the long awaited Prom which never came to be! The war had broken out just as they were about to finish high school, shattering their dreams and leaving them with an unfulfilled longing. But tonight, nothing will stop them. They will laugh, reminisce, and bask in the warmth of each other's company, grateful for the chance to reconnect and rekindle the bonds that had once been so strong.

———

As Besa slowly opened her eyes, she realised she was still tired. The weight of her nightmare lingered heavily upon her. However, her senses were awakened by the tantalising aroma of freshly made Turkish coffee and roasted peppers coming from the kitchen. She felt her heart fill with warmth. It was this scent that always reminded her of home, of the place where she belonged. It was a symbol of her mother's love and care, a reminder of the happy memories that they had shared together. Without hesitation, Besa rose from her bed and quickly made it, gathering her hair into a ponytail as she went. She knew that her mother would be in the kitchen, preparing breakfast and humming to the tune of the old folk songs that filled the air. As she entered the small kitchen, she saw her mother standing over the stove, working with an effortless grace that only mothers possess.

The sunlight streamed through the window, casting a warm glow on the kitchen table where a small radio was playing softly in the background. It was the same old radio with the broken antenna from which they had listened to the BBC and Voice of America during the war but now it played music from the local radio and mixed with the sizzle of the peppers, creating a symphony that filled Besa's heart with joy.

As she approached her mother, she felt a sense of peace and love wash over her. She wrapped her arms around her mother, hugging her tightly, and breathed in the familiar scent of home. Her mother looked up at her with eyes full of adoration and asked, "Did you sleep well?" Besa smiled and replied, "Yes, I slept wonderfully." She didn't want to worry her mother with tales of her nightmares or the restlessness that had plagued her sleep. Instead, she kissed her mother's hand gently and held it close to her heart. She noticed the fragility of her once-vibrant mother. Her hands now frail and nearly translucent, bore the marks of time - skin paper thin and delicate to the touch. Besa knew that her long absence had taken its toll on her mother's accelerated journey towards the inevitable march of ageing. Despite her best efforts during their long phone conversations, to reassure her mother that she was safe and flourishing in the US, the elderly woman couldn't help but worry incessantly about her daughter's well-being. She kissed her mother's hands again with love; hands that had tirelessly laboured to raise her with love and care and even though fragile looking now, still remained strong and gentle at the same time. Besa's strong connection with her mother endured, fueled by her mother's insistence on daily or near- daily phone calls. In the span of twenty years, there was perhaps only one occasion when Besa went three days without reaching out - a memory she'd rather forget. Her mother had scolded her, tears of worry flowing through the phone line, accusing Besa of insensitivity. Her mother confessed she couldn't sleep or eat if Besa failed to call at least every other day, and the thought of her unanswered calls would probably make her mother extremely distressed.

The bitter memory of that unforgotten, chilly Spring day in 1999 still lingered in Besa's mind. Everything in this apartment now reminded her of that day.

They had been rushed out of here, out of their city, and out of their country and uprooted in an instant. Looking back, she knew that it was only through the unwavering fearlessness and determination of her mother that Besa and her father were saved from certain doom on that day. Her mother's hand had never let go of Besa's hand, not even for one second, providing a steady anchor in the storm of chaos, guiding them through the crowds of people, like a compass guiding a boat at sea in a terrible storm.

Amid their frenzied escape, they had managed to gather a few meagre belongings and hastily pack them into an old suitcase. But what does one take when faced with only two options - to flee or to perish? The cacophony of shouts, insults, and door bangs had reverberated in their ears and the menacing threat of machine guns had loomed over them. She had tried to pack quickly while her mother pleading with her to hurry up and gather life necessities only added to her mounting anxiety. Her mind had seemed to be shut off and her body was in excruciating pain. She had pretended in front of her parents that nothing out of the ordinary had happened to her. She had passed out in the bed she had told her mother and the soldiers were trying to revive her and rush her out of her room. She didn't have time to think as everything had happened so fast, so haphazardly, so unexplainable. She had rushed to the bathroom and vomited violently. She felt void of any feelings or capacity to think. They were ordered to leave and they were waiting for everyone to move quickly out of their homes. They should feel lucky to be alive, her mother had said while trying to rush her and her father through the door.

But what were these life necessities that could be contained within the confines of a suitcase? That cold morning, she could not think of anything to take with her. She needed everything! Every item represented a part of her being. Each piece of clothing, every trinket, held a memory, a feeling, a part of her soul. Her heart had ached as she had looked at her fancy dress hanging in her closet, a beautiful creation made by the seamstress next door. It was meant for the upcoming Prom Night, an event she had eagerly anticipated. She knew she would never get to wear that dress because school and Prom Night had been cancelled. Their whole lives were cancelled! When she left most of her things behind that day, she realised they had not been mere objects, but an extension of herself. They had represented who she was, who she had been, and who she had hoped to become. That cold spring morning, their world had crumbled in just a matter of moments, and she had stood there, staring at her mother with awe and admiration as she frantically had packed their belongings. The precision with which her mother worked, as though she had foreseen this day, left Besa in a state of wonder. Her father on the other hand was defeated, aged beyond his years in just one day, as Besa looked at him in despair. Her mother had transformed into a fearless lioness that exuded strength and resilience, unshaken by the looming threat of the paramilitaries. Besa had felt lost while her body was failing to obey the commands of the brain to move quickly, tears streaming down her face, obscuring her vision while her mother had dressed her in layers of warm clothes, knowing fully well that the biting cold of that early morning would be their constant companion in the days to come. As they hurried out of their apartment, Besa had clutched her ID that her mother handed her and a little sum of money that her mother had divided between them, feeling frightened to the core at the prospect of being separated from her parents. Only her mother's unwavering determination and fierce spirit had given her a glimmer of hope. She had watched with awe as her mother's superhuman strength pushed them forward as they had joined their neighbours in a frantic dash down the stairs.

The lines of people walking with guns pointed at them, had stretched for miles and miles. They didn't know where they were going. They didn't know what was lying in wait for them. They didn't know whether they would ever come back home.

It was only her mother's hand, holding her hand tightly that assured her there was still hope. The whole world, the entirety of love and protection in the world was in her mother's hand, in that hand that was both strong and gentle at the same time. She only remembered the powerful love in that clench of her mother's hand and that was all she had left from any sense of normality in the world.

She remembered how frightened she had been that day and how her heart had raced constantly as she had gazed upon the scenes unfolding before her. Once they were out on the streets of the city, a sea of people stripped of their identity and dignity, trudged forward with heads bowed and hearts heavy. The weight of the oppression they endured was palpable in the air, suffocating and oppressive. In all that crowd there were no sounds. It was a screaming silence. The only sounds that Besa heard that day were the cries of frightened children, their small voices piercing the stillness with heart-breaking despair. Like a herd being led to slaughter and accepting their fate with their heads bowed down, they shuffled along in silence.

"Look down," her mother told her. "Don't look them in the eye. Don't let them see your face." Keep Walking! Walk!"

That tumultuous day had been etched into Besa's memory with vividness that had refused to fade for many years, no matter how much she tried to forget it. But now all that remained in her memory were the feet, countless feet, shod in muddy shoes, stumbling and slipping in the sodden ground. The elderly faltered and struggled, while women carried their wailing infants and clutched their children's hands tightly, desperate to avoid any contact with soldiers and police or to attract their attention. And in the middle of it all, the cold was a constant, biting presence that seemed to seep into every bone. For Besa, the frigid air seemed to be a physical manifestation of the despair and uncertainty that filled the air that day. Her whole being had felt frozen from the trauma and emotions.

The only warmth came from her mother's hand, holding hers tightly. The immensity of the universe, the entire expanse of love and kindness, lay within the grasp of her mother's hand as they were led towards the trains, overfilled with people. They were told to leave and never to come back. The trains took them to the border with North Macedonia and away from everything that was dear to them.

Her mother's strength was a revelation for Besa, surpassing her imagination that she could have perceived her mother to be. The determination to ensure her and her father's safety was nothing short of extraordinary - a force that seemed otherworldly. In that moment, her mother had appeared larger than life, transcending her usual gentle demeanour. Confined by societal norms, her mother had never shown such defiance, always adhering to the expectations of an obedient wife and mother. Despite her adulthood, she harboured childlike insecurities and hesitated to make decisions regarding family matters. Yet, on that fateful day, her mother seized control, resolute in her mission to protect her family and get them to safety with the focus of a lioness protecting her young. Amidst the chaos engulfing her world, all the familiarity of life as Besa had known it before that day, condensed into the warmth of her mother's hand.

Two

ARIANA

Ariana lay in her bed, tossing and turning for what felt like hours. Sleep was elusive, and her thoughts were consumed with problems large and small. Frustrated, she rose from her bed and made her way to the tiny balcony of her bedroom, where she lit up a cigarette. As she inhaled deeply, the smoke filled her lungs, and her mind began to calm. She gazed out at the quiet night, the stars twinkling above her, and the city lights below. Her eyes shifted back to the bedroom, where her faithful cat, Mic (Mitz), lay sleeping at the foot of her bed. She watched Mic's peaceful breathing and longed for a sense of calm within herself. She was grateful for Mic's unwavering presence in her life, a reminder that despite her feelings of lonliness, she was never truly alone. With a heavy heart, Ariana took another drag of her cigarette and exhaled slowly, the smoke rising into the night sky. She knew she needed to find a way to calm her racing thoughts and get some rest, but for now, she was content to stand there, watching over Mic as he slept peacefully.

'Ah, why can't I be as blissfully content and carefree as he is?', she thought to herself. Mic, the creamy coloured cat with orange patches, was more than just a pet to Ariana. He was her faithful companion, her confidante and her only family. She had found him on a cold rainy day, two years ago, outside her apartment building, shivering and meowing weakly. The cat had looked at her with pleading eyes, as if he knew that she was the only one who could help him. Ariana had been lost and lonely for a long time, searching for something to fill the void in her soul and when she looked into Mic's eyes, she saw something that she had been missing for so long- love and compassion. Maybe it was the cat that saved her, and not the other way around. She was sure of that now. From that day on, Mic became her constant companion. He would curl up next to her on the couch as she read or watched TV, or nuzzle against her when she cried. He never judged her, never asked for anything in return. He was simply there, a source of comfort and solace in the world that felt cold and uncaring. The day that she found Mic, Ariana had knocked on all her neighbours' doors, asking if the cat belonged to anyone. She did that out of courtesy towards the cat and not her neighbours. When no one claimed it, she happily took the cat home and never separated from it again. It was hard to explain to anyone how much she loved that cat. She couldn't wait to come home to him every evening. In him, she had found a friend, a companion, a family. A living creature that somehow understood her without asking questions or judging her in any way.

She would do anything to keep the cat safe and happy and she believed Mic would do the same for her. At the point in her life when she had found the cat, she had felt like she had forgotten how loving someone felt. She had lived with a constant sense of emptiness ever since the war and loneliness was tearing her apart like a tempestuous storm raging within her soul. The scars of loss and heartache were engraved deep within Ariana's being. The memories of the dearest people in her life that she had loved and lost haunted her every waking moment. Her world that had been shattered by a violent upheaval, her country torn apart by conflict and chaos left her feeling lost for many years.

The cat purred loudly, and Ariana smiled looking at it. She pulled the balcony door towards herself, closing it, to not disturb the cat. She could not imagine her life without Mic. She lifted the cigarette to her lips, inhaling deeply and savouring the acrid smoke as it filled her lungs. With a resigned sigh, she took one last drag before extinguishing the glowing ember against the overflowing ashtray on her balcony. As she stubbed out the cigarette, she couldn't ignore the nagging voice in the back of her mind, reminding her that she smoked too much. The thought of quitting loomed ever-present, but the more she dwelled on it, the more she found herself reaching for another cigarette. Every evening, as she smoked her cigarettes her in her small balcony and gazed out at the world beyond it, whether it was cold in winter or sunny in summertime, she kept thinking about her past but still, after all these years, not being able to clearly picture her future. She struggled to envisage herself as an old woman, the idea feeling foreign and unsettling. The truth was, she wasn't even sure if she wanted to live long enough to see herself grow old. Perhaps that was why she smoked so relentlessly, a way to dull the fear and uncertainty of the passing years.

It was late and the city had settled into a quiet stillness. It seemed like everyone in the building had already gone to sleep. As was her habit, she remained awake long into the night, the silence of the world outside offering much needed peace from her hectic days. For her, sleep was a rare commodity, a luxury that was afforded only in small, fleeting moments. She could hardly recall a time when she had slept for more than a few hours in one stretch.

Amid her usual anguish that plagued her every waking moment, this night she couldn't shake the sense of unease that had settled in her gut. She went to lay in bed but her mind was consumed by the decision she had made to attend her high school reunion party. It had seemed like a good idea at the time, a chance to reconnect with old friends and revisit a time in her life that felt like a distant memory.

What was she thinking agreeing to attend an event that was so far removed from the life that she now led? So many years had passed since high school, it felt like another lifetime, a world inhabited by a person that was no longer her. It was as if the person who had lived those years was someone else entirely, a child who bore little resemblance to the woman she was now.

She had promised her friend Besa that she would be there and now she couldn't walk back on her word. Besa came all the way from the US to attend the party and she just couldn't let her go to the festivities alone, especially for the reason that she might feel like a foreigner or a guest after spending all these years abroad. On the other hand, she knew she herself couldn't ignore the pull of the past, the desire to revisit a time when she was a different person.

Had she been too hasty in agreeing to attend? Should she have taken more time to consider the implications of confronting the ghosts of her past by meeting all her High School Friends that knew about her tragedies of the past and how she had struggled to get over them. Could she pretend like nothing had happened to that 19 year old that she was twenty years ago and attend a party, a celebration of an era that she didn't really want to be reminded of ?

She has spent years trying to bury the memories of her past, to forget the pain and trauma that had left her scarred and broken and she knew that the slightest scratch on the surface of her seemingly uneventful life could send her spiralling back into the darkness, the memories and emotions running back to overwhelm her.

She had tried everything -therapy, meditation, self-care but nothing could erase the scars that marked her soul.

Every time that she heard the word high school, she thought of Arben.

It seemed that not a day went by without him crossing her mind, even if just for a moment. Sometimes she would spend hours lost in thought, recalling every aspect of him - from the curve of his smile to the sound of his laughter. With each passing day, she clung to these memories with increasing desperation, as if the very act of remembering could bring him back to her. For her, the memory of him was a treasure, a priceless gem that she could not afford to lose. She longed for him in the quiet moments when the world was still, and she was left alone with her thoughts. With her eyes closed she conjured up every detail of his being: his curly, messy, long brown hair, that fell haphazardly around his face, his sparkling almond intelligent eyes that seemed to hold the universe within them, his warm and bright smile with slightly crooked teeth that always made her heart skip a beat. She would close her eyes and allow herself to be consumed by the memory of him, to be lost in the vision of him, relishing the way memories enveloped her like a warm embrace. In those moments she felt like she could almost touch his face. This ritual of embarking on the journey to his memory, a pilgrimage she made with the reverence of a devout believer, was her lifeline, a lifeline she clung onto with every fibre of her being. She knew without a doubt that her sanity and her very existence depended on it. To forget him, to let go of the memories they had shared, was to lose a part of herself that she could never get back. She was haunted by the fear that one day, she would forget how he looked, how he smiled, how he laughed or how he spoke. And with that loss, she feared, would come the unravelling of her very existence.

She wasn't really living now, not in the way that mattered

because every new day was a step further from him and a step closer to the continuous lonely life that she was afraid of. Her heart still lived in the days long gone, when they had walked hand in hand, and shared their hopes and dreams with each other. It was in those memories that she found solace, in those moments that she felt truly alive.

She also remembered their conversations, the jokes that he had told her, the way he had teased her sometimes with his good natured humour and the sound of his laughter ringing in her ears like a sweet melody. She was meticulous in her recollection, as if she were carefully storing away precious clips of her past life, categorising them in her mind like a librarian organising a library. She would open those files on her mind, dust them off, and bask in their warmth like a fire on a cold winter's night and when she was done, she would put them back gently, carefully as if they were fragile artefacts that needed to be preserved for all eternity. These memories were the one thing that nothing and no one could take away from her as long as she lived and as long as she remembered.

She closed her eyes once more, listening to Mic's purring next to her feet.

She only had one photo of Arben, which she did not really like. The picture was far from ideal. It was his ID card photo, a mundane snapshot taken without any thought or care, and it did not capture the essence of who Arben truly was.

Arben's mother had taken it upon herself to have the photo enlarged and framed, and it now hung prominently on the wall of his mother's home and another one, not as large, in a simple black frame, stood on top of her bookshelves. She often found herself staring at it, trying to discern some hidden truth in Arben's stoic expression.

In the picture, he was staring directly into the camera, his face devoid of emotion, his demeanour serious and unyielding. It was a stark contrast to the vibrant and lively person that Ariana knew him to be, a young man bursting with energy and always quick with a smile. She couldn't help but feel that this photo did not do him justice, that it failed to capture even a fraction of the warmth and vitality that he exuded.

She knew that if Arben was still with them, he would not have wanted his photo splashed across newspapers and social media platforms, a macabre reminder of the past. Every year since the liberation, the world mourned and remembered, calling for justice for the victims and the missing of the last war in Kosovo and Ariana couldn't help but wonder what Arben would have thought of it all. She was sure he would have been proud of the way people were coming together to seek accountability and closure but he wouldn't like his photo being shown everywhere as a symbol of pain and loss. The photo was a bleak and empty image that revealed nothing of the young man she had loved. Every time Ariana gazed upon it, her heart heavy with the weight of her loss she murmured the same things to herself "It doesn't say anything. It doesn't show anything about him." To Ariana, the photo was little more than a grim reminder of the war that had claimed so many. The man in the image looked like just another missing victim, lost among the countless others who had disappeared into the darkness. She wanted him to be more than just another faceless casualty. It was a selfish desire, perhaps, but Ariana longed for him to be special, even in death. She wanted the world to know the depth of his love for life, his dreams and ambitions, the unique intelligence and boundless energy that set him apart from the rest. Above all, she wanted everyone to know how deeply he had loved her. But the photo could not capture the way he had laughed, the determination that had burned in his eyes, or his fierce passion. It could not convey the depth of his love, nor the brilliant mind that lay behind his eyes.

As she looked upon the empty image, Ariana could not help but agree with her own thoughts; ID photos were useless when it came to representing the true essence of a person. They were nothing more than hollow shells, devoid of the life and energy that made a person unique.

———

Ariana remembered precisely the very first moment she saw Arben.

"Everyone say hello to the new student!" the Language Teacher had announced, her words hung in the air echoing through the bustling classroom. As her eyes swept through the crowded classroom, searching for the unknown newcomer, she suddenly caught sight of him. She remembered that moment with exact accuracy, the moment when her eyes met his for the very first time. He looked different from the rest, more mature, almost out of place. But it was his smile that really caught her attention, lighting up his entire face and making his eyes sparkle like diamonds. His curly, messy long hair gave him a pop star look that was intriguing and captivating. He was tall, hunching his back slightly, looking at everyone through his curls, a shy smile playing on his lips. And when he raised his hand in greeting and introduced himself, something stirred within her. She couldn't help but smile, for his smile was contagious, filling her with warmth and joy. She came to love many things about him over time, but it was that infectious smile that captured her heart from the very start. Ariana had plunged headlong into the depths of love for Arben long before he had uttered a single word to her. In fact, well before he had ever taken notice of her, she had already fallen for him with an intensity that defied every explanation. To her, Arben was a beacon of light, shining as brightly as the sun itself. Ariana's heart would skip a beat, and her cheeks would flush with warmth every time she stole a secret glance at him from afar. She was irresistibly drawn to the magnetic warmth of his presence. Despite the enduring teasing and bullying as a new student, Arben remained unfazed, keeping his gaze fixed on the books he immersed himself in during recess and in between bell rings. His dedication to reading literature left Ariana fascinated. In all her years, she had never encountered a boy who was so utterly consumed by books. To Ariana, he was a refreshing and intriguing enigma, a boy whose love for books had ignited her own curiosity and captured her heart.

She had tried to get Arben's attention for weeks, without success. But then her friend, Besa, with whom she shared a desk had an idea. "Get yourself a book and read it during recess," she suggested. "He'll take interest in the book and then you can weave your charm". Besa had brought her a huge, heavy book from her father's library the next day. It was a weighty volume detailing the exploits of an Albanian hero named Mic Sokoli, who had bravely fought against the Ottoman Empire.

"Why such a massive book?" Ariana had complained

"Well, my dear", Besa had jested, "for a grander impact. He won't be able to ignore you reading this".

Ariana was not one to be enthralled by patriotic literature, or to keep herself up to date with the news. She did not participate in student protests, nor did she engage in political discussions. In many ways, she was much like her father.

Ariana's father harboured a deep-seated aversion to politics and would always try to avoid listening to the news. However, in their country of Kosovo, this proved to be a perpetual struggle. Despite his best efforts, he could not entirely escape the tumultuous currents of the political upheaval.

As the eldest of four siblings, Ariana held a special place in her father's heart. He even affectionately referred to her as "my son", a term of endearment that Albanian parents used when expressing deep love and respect for their daughters. Her father, a factory worker, believed that hard physical labour and practical skills made people happy and successful. "The less people involve themselves in intellectual work, the happier their life will be.", he often declared. They didn't have any books at home. They were a luxury that they couldn't afford. Ariana's father possessed an unwavering honesty and a heart of pure gold. He often felt out of place in their small apartment, as he had grown up in a picturesque village near Prishtina, surrounded by nature. He would often travel to visit his extended family in the village, seeking solace in the simplicity of rural life. Ariana cherished her father's gentle nature and gratitude, recalling memories of his kind spirit. He exuded a perpetual air of contentment, never missing an opportunity to express his gratitude about life and everything else, with unwavering sincerity. Each day, he shared his profound appreciation with those around him, and especially with Ariana and her siblings, for whom he bore an open and genuine affection.

Ariana had never again been able to find that same sense of security, clarity and positivity that her father's perspective on life had instilled in her when she was a child. Ariana's mother, a quiet and unassuming woman of delicate beauty, devoted herself tirelessly to the upbringing of their four children. Though she had a deep affection for her ungainly husband, she never expressed it publicly. Her love for him seemed confined solely to her gaze, when she occasionally cast shy glances at her husband. Throughout their many years of marriage and the raising of their children, Ariana never once saw her parents embrace, let alone kiss or show any physical affection in front of their children or anyone else. Such displays were simply not customary for parents of their time. Whenever Ariana caught her parents exchanging furtive smiles and glances, a palpable current of electricity crackled between them. She delighted in watching them blush like lovestruck teenagers and beam at each other with adoration.

Years later, the memory of those moments of pure familial love continued to evoke a sense of profound happiness within Ariana. Even now, she could not help but smile at the thought of her parents' deep devotion to each other. Though Ariana did not follow any particular religious doctrine, she often found herself wondering if her parents' spirits still roamed the halls of their former apartment. Did they continue to watch over her even now, long after their physical bodies had departed this world? She wondered how they had died. Had they been given a chance to look into each other's eyes one last time before their execution? Or had they been forced to watch their children, Ariana's siblings, get shot first? When she sought answers after the war, Ariana was told that her entire family had been brutally executed in a single day. She was told they had been lined up against a featureless wall along the small road and they were mercilessly gunned down by paramilitaries, their bodies riddled with endless rounds of bullets.

It may sound weird but she was glad they all died at the same time. The thought that they didn't see each other suffer brought her a bit of comfort. The thought that their suffering lasted only a few minutes gave her some kind of concolation. She told herself, they might have not even had time to realise what was happening.

This was some very strange consolation, she thought, feeling immense guilt about the fact that she could be 'happy' about her family's death in any shape or form. She thought she was strange for thinking that way and she felt like her mind had come up with this kind of thinking by itself somehow to protect her from going mad.

Ariana yearned for closure. She longed to find the remains of her loved ones and honour their memory with the dignity they deserved. She yearned to lay their bodies to rest, adorn their graves with beautiful plaques, and lay flowers on them.

Her mother loved flowers so much. The balcony of their home had always been adorned with an array of blossoming plants of all kinds, from the early spring all the way through to the last days of autumn. It was a beautiful garden, meticulously tended to by her mother, which lent the entire building a cheerful air.

The thought that the bodies of her loved ones might be inside one of the many mass graves that were still being unearthed, 20 years after the war, or in the bottom of a lake or river somewhere in Serbia, where the bodies of dead civilians were taken in freezer trucks that had carried them there all the way from Kosovo to conceal the evidence of the massacres; the thought of their fate, of their unknown resting place, filled her with zombie-like despair while at the same time stoking an unquenchable inferno of fury. She had been advised to try and transform her raging fury into a force for good. She was counselled that clinging to her anger would not alter the past, it would not resurrect those she had lost. She was told that anger was an irrational emotion that would only consume her from within, a poison that would corrode her very being. The remedy they proposed was simple: count to ten, to a hundred, before reacting, practice breathing exercises, meditation.

"Time will heal you," they whispered, their voices heavy with empathy.

Yet, despite their well-intentioned advice, Ariana listened politely, but did not truly believe a word they said. The gaping wound that had been carved into her soul remained as raw as on the day it was inflicted. The notion that the passage of time would simply heal the wound seemed like a cruel and thoughtless lie. She remained unconvinced by the words of those who sought to offer her solace.

The day Ariana received word that the remains of her loved ones may have been uncovered in a mass grave, she knew that she could not allow the heinous crime against her family go without due consequence for those who had committed it. As the sole survivor, she felt it was her duty to fight for justice for herself, for Arben, and for the memory of her family. She vowed to not settle for anything less than justice, for the peace of mind and closure that she and her family deserved. Yet as the years passed, and the wheels of justice turned slowly, Ariana's patience wore thin. Twenty years had passed, and still, there was no closure in sight. The wait seemed endless, and the thought that the perpetrators of such unspeakable acts of violence were still at large gnawed her heart and mind from the moment she opened her eyes in the morning until she closed them late at night.

Searching through the hundreds of human remains unearthed from the massive graves was an event when she felt something yet more profound changed within her. It was like she had a real reckoning with her past. She had rushed to the place where they told her to go and her heart and mind had pounded heavily with a strange hope that she would finally be able to identify her parents and siblings. That day, she decided to stop grieving in the way she had been until then. Something changed within her. A force that she never knew she had awakened within her. She still wasn't sure where that "awakening" came from. Was it somehow wired into people in order to accommodate the triumph and continuation of life? Was it growing up and becoming an adult, realising that her parents and siblings were gone and there was nothing she could do to bring them back. "The living must go on living," an old woman walking next to her told her. "There's nothing we can do my dear and you are young, you should accept and go on living". The old woman was truly concerned about her. She walked close to her and offered her her hand. They continued looking through the body bags, holding their hands. The old lady never stopped with the comforting words that continued to play in her head for days to come.

As Ariana stood amidst the crowd of people searching for their missing loved ones, she realised that she'd been a coward. Moping around and feeling sorry for herself was embarrassing, she thought, especially when everyone else around her was also affected by the devastating consequences of war. She stood in the crowd of grieving individuals, all searching for the remains of their loved ones, and she couldn't help but feel overwhelmed by the powerful emotions in the air. Mothers, fathers, and grandparents alike were scouring among the white body bags that were lined up row after row inside a huge tent. Tattered clothes lay next to some of the bags, a grim reminder of the loved ones who were no longer there to claim them. A faded sweater, a leather jacket, a pair of sneakers; they all represented the dead, waiting to be recognized by a family member. Together with the others, she searched through every bag, feeling numb. What other emotion could she possibly have while taking part in this bizarre ritual of witnessing human savagery. She was brought up to believe that "right" and "wrong" were instincts that were instilled into human beings from birth, that morality was something that came naturally to human beings. But then this... She could not find the right words to describe. As the reality of the situation set in, her numbness gave way to all-consuming anger, a fiery rage that kept her awake for days. She couldn't sleep, she couldn't eat, she couldn't go out of the house or talk to anyone. She just lingered on her couch in the living room drifting away on and off in a haze.

As she left the tent that day, Ariana carried with her the weight of the world on her shoulders. The possibility that her family's remains might never be identified, that justice might never be served, was crushing her. The burning anger inside her added more fuel to her determination to do something, anything, to honour her loved ones and ensure that no one else suffered the same fate ever again. A few gruelling weeks after that event which felt as if it had been the hardest episode in her life at that point, a time when she felt totally hopeless, by chance or miracle, Ariana had a realisation - that grieving should be dignified, and that the dead deserved to be honoured and respected with stoicism. No longer did she want to wallow in her own sorrow, but instead, she vowed to approach the situation with grace and reverence for those who had been taken too soon. She refused to be a victim any longer. "We must live" the words of the old lady echoed in her mind.

Joining the new Kosovo Police Force was her way of taking back control and seeking the justice her family deserved. Through gruelling training, she regained not only her physical strength but also her sense of purpose and dignity. It was a chance for her to serve her country and make a difference, to fight for the justice and peace that had been denied to so many. And for Ariana, it was the only way to truly honour the memory of her family and Arben and to find some peace in a world that had taken so much from her. She resolved to honour her family's and Arben's memory by fighting for justice, not just for herself but for all those who had suffered. It was time to stop waiting and start acting.

THREE

SUZI

As Suzi reached for her phone, her mind raced with excitement for the upcoming Reunion Party. With eager anticipation, she carefully checked her calendar, verifying the time of her hair and makeup appointment the following day. It was essential that tomorrow evening, she arrived at the party looking her best, but not be there too early, as she didn't want to risk ruining her carefully crafted look before the fun even began. At the same time, she couldn't be too late either, she thought, lest she missed the grand entrance of her friends and acquaintances. After much deliberation, she had decided on a 4:30 pm appointment, hoping it would strike the perfect balance between style and punctuality for the 7pm start of the evening's festivities. With a satisfied smile, she flicked her phone onto "do not disturb", eager to rest tonight, to have a good sleep and prepare herself for the next day.

She sighed and lowered the phone, the image of her slightly

swollen face that she saw a few minutes ago on her phone screen now bothering her a little bit.

She couldn't help but feel a bit self-conscious and insecure, wondering if anyone at the upcoming party tomorrow night would notice her latest botox treatment.

Suzi was a beautiful woman. Her hair always neat and blow dried with perfect hues of blond highlights and her blue eyes and a charming smile exuded kindness, elegance, warmth and compassion. She admitted to herself that she was afraid of losing her beautiful features with age. Uncarachterystically for her, she realised that recently she was afraid of not being liked anymore by her friends and acquaintances, her large social circle that buzzed around her all the time. She couldn't bear criticism of any kind. Her husband's cruel words echoed in her head, and she could feel the anger building up inside her every time she thought about them. How dare he make derogatory comments about her appearance, even in fits of anger or when he wanted to wound her deeply. Why did it matter so much to him whether she resembled a 'Serbian' or not? He had objections with her stubbornness he had said that resembled that of a Serbian. Suzi's mother was Serbian and he had found a way to make her angry by pointing out that fact to make it sound like a character flaw. Or was it that he had found her vulnerability; her inner struggle with identity and belonging and her constant need, since the war with Serbia ended, for her to prove herself amongst her compatriots in liberated Kosovo.

She opened her phone again and switched the camera on. As she looked at herself on the screen, she couldn't help but wonder how she had ended up in this loveless, toxic marriage. Their constant bickering had turned into full-blown arguments, and the insults they hurled at each other had become more hurtful and nonsensical with each passing day. She had tried to reason with him, to make him understand that the differences between Serbs and Albanians were insignificant in the grand scheme of things. But Bashkim had never been one to listen to reason, insisting that it was possible to tell the difference between the two ethnicities and that everyone could tell that she was "mixed". He attributed her defiance, her sense of entitlement, her constant desire for attention, and even her reluctance to do household chores to what he termed as cultural traits inherited from her Serbian mother.

She shook her head, dismissing these irrational thoughts. She refused to let Bashkim's hurtful words, spoken in anger and without consideration, undermine her confidence. Everyday, she worked on improving herself and tried to bolster her confidence and her sense of self-worth but it seemed Bashkim knew exactly how to hurt her feelings. She felt relieved after their separation, no longer subjected to his simmering anger and frustration, which had grown unbearable over the years. While he wasn't physically violent, he carried within him a constant sense of irritation and dissatisfaction with life. Emotionally volatile and needy, he seemed constantly exhausted, depressed and quick to anger. "It's PTSD from the war," one of her friends had suggested. "My husband is going through the same thing". "I don't know what we are going to do?" Suzi had replied. "Men often refuse mental health treatment".

She didn't dare open the topic of mental health check or treatment with Bashkim. She feared he would interpret it as an insult, believing she was implying he was "crazy", which would only poke his anger further. She was terrified of what he might do if his anger escalated or what actions he might take if provoked further.

Taking a deep breath, she powered off her phone trying to calm down her mind. She tried to focus on envisioning a perfect hairstyle and flawless makeup for the upcoming reunion party. After a few moments, she reached for her phone camera again, scrutinising her slightly swollen face in the camera's reflection. Her mother's features inherited by her were evident in her beautiful face, and she had inherited her fathers infectious smile. She refused to entertain the notion that her appearance defined her nationality. To her, there was no distinction between the physical attributes of the two Balkan nations - no variation in skin tone, no inherent traits that set them apart. It was all a construct of people's perceptions, she thought. She was just as much Albanian as she was Serbian.

Living in a country where the tension between the two groups were palpable, Suzi had grown accustomed to being labelled as not sufficiently belonging to either community. She knew that if she lived in Belgrade, someone would have pointed out her Albanian heritage. It was a tiresome and hurtful existence when she allowed it to bother her, but she refused to let these mindless nationalists ruin her life. Suzi silently vowed to never let anyone's opinions or biases undermine her sense of self. She embraced her individuality as Suzi, refusing to be swayed by nationalist rhetoric that sought to pigeon hole her into one nationality or the other. To her, generalisations were harmful; she believed that people were people, each with their complexities and nuances, regardless of their heritage or language. Good and bad existed in everyone so she would continue to judge individuals based on their actions and their character and not their nationality, exactly like she was taught by her parents.

She still couldn't sleep and opened her phone once more. Like every other time when she had trouble falling asleep, she started scrolling through the old photographs on her phone and immediately felt a warmth of nostalgia wash over her.

Each image that she looked at was a treasured memory, a precious moment from a time long gone. She had carefully selected the best photos from the countless albums and photographs piled in shoe boxes that her family had collected over the years and she had carefully, over a long period of time, photographed them one by one to keep them all safe in her digital collection. She had saved them in a special folder on her phone that she opened often before bed. They were her most prized possessions, the only things she had left of her family after the war had taken everything else. As she gazed at the faded images, a complex mix of emotions washed over her. There was a sense of distance from her past, mingled with nostalgia and a complete detachment from the photos themselves. The figures captured in the frames - her parents and brother- appeared like strangers from another world. She could recall the moments captured in each picture vividly, yet they seemed more like scenes from a movie or fragments from a dream rather than events she had truly lived or participated in. Time had moved too fast, she thought. The years had slipped away in a blink of an eye. The frozen moments in these photographs seemed like they were from a different lifetime. She felt a sense of loss for the time that had passed, and the memories that had faded away.

She looked at her parents' engagement photograph and felt so much love for both of them. She missed them a lot. Suzi's mother and father had fallen in love as young university students in Belgrade in the early 1970s. They married soon after graduation and settled in Kosovë to raise a family. She deeply cherished the memory of her parents and of the country that didn't exist anymore; Yugoslavia. She longed for the way things used to be. She marvelled at the elegance and beauty of her parents, whose poise in those old photographs, resembled that of Hollywood stars. The backdrops of the snapshots were captivating, showcasing the grandeur of Belgrade's buildings, the beauty of Kosovo's nature, and the allure of Croatia's beaches. As Suzi looked at these photos, she always thought about how good her life once was. Her idyllic existence had vanished in a blink of an eye, leaving Suzi struggling to comprehend how everything had unravelled so quickly. In a mere matter of weeks, she lost her family, her country, and nearly her own life and the world fell apart before her eyes. The suddenness of it all left her shocked and disoriented, as she had never expected such a rapid and devastating upheaval.

She vividly recalled the early Spring day in '99, walking alone in the forest, fleeing for her life, while everything around her was burning. Since that harrowing experience, she vowed to never take anything for granted , not even the simplest decisions in life, whose long term consequences can sometimes be unimaginable. Even now, she couldn't shake off the "what ifs" that plagued her mind. What if she had gone away to Belgrade with her mother when she had the chance? What if they had all left the country in time? What if her parents had saved them all by just packing and moving away to go anywhere, instead of waiting and believing for things to get better in this country? Why didn't her parents think this through? She still blamed them. They would have probably all been alive and well living in some peaceful country. But no! Her father would have never considered such an act as anything but cowardice.

———

Few months before she found herself running for her life across borders, as snowflakes fell softly on the window sill, Suzi sat next to her brother Alex, trying to focus on the movie they were watching. Her mind kept drifting off to the new boy in her class, and she found herself daydreaming instead. They didn't even pay attention when their mother entered the living room, dressed in a coat with a carrying bag in her hands. "I have to go," their mother suddenly interrupted, requesting their attention. Suzi and Alex turned to her, surprised. Their mother was usually calm and collected and seeing her in tears was a shock. "Go where?" Alex asked, his confusion evident. "I can't live here anymore," their mother cried. "It is unbearable for me." They didn't know how to react and looking back, she remembered that they didn't really think much of it. Or maybe it was only Suzi who didn't think much of it. They both hugged their mother, unsure of what to do or say. Alex, who was more grown and mature than her, reverted to a childlike state in the presence of their mother's distress. "We're coming with you!" he declared, holding their mother's hands.

"I hate the political situation here," Alex ranted, his voice shaking with emotion. "The constant demonstrations at the university, the news... I hate how my Albanian friends look at me, and how my Serbian friends are avoiding me. Why can't Dad just quit politics and take us all to Belgrade?"

Their mother tried to reason with them but they were both stubborn in their opposite requests. Suzi was determined to finish high school and attend her prom and she wouldn't hear of leaving, while Alex refused to stay in a place where he felt ostracised. Their mother seemed to be perplexed and indecisive too.

She pleaded with Alex to reconsider, warning him of the dangers that lay outside of their home. However Alex was headstrong and determined to leave, even suggesting changing his last name as soon as he arrived in Serbia to distance himself from the Albanian identity he felt burdened by. In his view it was the Albanians who were responsible for all the turmoil, demanding greater rights and equality in a society he believed to be faultless from within his sheltered bubble. Suzi held her mother tight, embracing her with a sense of relief that she wasn't going with her. She was sure her mother would return in a few days, as she had gone to visit her parents in Belgrade before without them. Her mother's emotional farewell didn't quite resonate with Suzi, who didn't give much thought to what she thought to be only temporary separation. Little did Suzi know that this would be the last time she would ever see her mother. The memory of their goodbye hug still lingered in her mind, now filled with a profound sadness and longing for a chance to say a proper goodbye.

That night, Suzi's father didn't return home either, occupied with endless meetings at the party headquarters. She watched him on television, on the evening news giving an impassioned speech about the importance of unity between Serbs and Albanians, urging calm amidst the chaos unfolding. As she watched her father on the screen, a momentary sense of panic crept over her, but she had pushed it away. Instead, she changed the channel, got some ice cream and thought about the upcoming day at school and the cute boy in her class that kept asking to borrow her fancy pencils.

Morning arrived, but Alex was nowhere to be found. Suzi frantically called her father in the office and her mother in Belgrade at her grandparents house. She reached out to all of Alex's friends, both Serbs and Albanians, hoping for any information. No one had any clues about his whereabouts, leaving Suzi feeling lost and alone in a world that was rapidly becoming unfamiliar and frightening.

————

March 1999

Suzi wept quietly on that cold March evening in 1999 within the old walls of her grandparents' home, in a tiny village approximately 10 kilometres away from the capital of Prishtina. It was so quiet and serene here that she felt afraid to go out of the house once the sun started to set. She hated the fact that her father had brought her here without respecting her wish to stay home in their apartment in the city. It was so quiet and peaceful here but she couldn't shake the feeling of an impending danger even though war never crossed her mind.

Perhaps, in her father's eyes, this small village where he had been born, was an idyllic paradise; the surrounding mountains and fields, still in the early stages of blooming, were a sight to behold. The little flowers that dotted the fields with their yellow and white hues, hinted at the arrival of Spring. But she only felt lonelier and more scared there. The village itself, with its old houses donning red roofs, was scattered across the valley, following the winding course of a small brook. During the day, the village was not as quiet but filled with the laughter of children running around before and after school, often congregating in groups outside the local store, either playing soccer or taking care of their animals. Spring was coming and everyone was happy about it.

Suzi's father dropped her off after a few days from her mother's departure for Belgarde and after Alex' disappearance. He had hurriedly hugged her, embraced his parents and left hurriedly in his official government car driven by his chauffeur, ignoring her pleas and tears. In this tranquil little village, where the stillness was so profound, one could hardly imagine the approaching calamity that war would soon bring, and now she guessed that was why her father had brought her here. But at that time she was angry with him and couldn't understand why her father had forced her to leave the comfort of her home and come and stay with her grandparents. She was content being alone at home in the apartment, and she missed her friends in the neighbourhood. The school was now closed indefinitely, her father told her. Absurd-she thought. The much-anticipated prom night, where she had hoped to make memories that would last a lifetime, was now just a dream and her dress lay abandoned in the closet, a sad reminder of what could have been. Despite this she still clung to hope that it would be a few weeks, a month perhaps when everything would go back to normal. She spoke to her mother on the phone the other day. Her mother assured her that everything would end soon, and she would be back. She also told her that Alex was safe and working for the government. Her mom insisted too that there was nothing to worry about. She urged Suzi to be patient and stay with her grandparents for a little while longer. But Suzi was impatient and she was livid with everyone, feeling alone and neglected, despite her grandmother's best efforts to lift her spirits.

Her grandmother knew how much Suzi loved fli (phlee, traditional Albanian pancake), and had lovingly prepared it for her today. Despite the exquisite layers of soft, creamy dough, grilled to perfection over the open flames, Suzi's mood remained sullen and sour. The (fli) failed to elevate her spirits and she was in a bad mood dwelling on how she's missing out on outings with her friends and missing the opportunity of seeing the guy that she liked. She could have seized the chance to spend time with him without her parents or Alex noticing. However, being isolated in this village with no nightlife, she felt like she was going stir - crazy. She tried to forget everything by going to bed early even though she knew she wouldn't be able to sleep.

As she lay there in the darkness, her thoughts consumed by the fear of missing out on her life, she looked out the window at the radiant moon, suspended like a precious gold medal in the inky blackness of the sky. The window in the room once belonging to her father, didn't have curtains, letting the moonlight spill into the room, illuminating her face and casting an ethereal glow across her surroundings.

The urge to flee this place and return to the familiarity of Prishtina gnawed at her. She decided to catch the first bus out in the morning, even if it meant doing so secretly from her grandparents. She was desperate to leave even if she was concerned about disappointing her grandparents and her father.

As Suzi lay there, her heart pounding in her chest, she tried to rationalise what she had just seen. Perhaps it was just her imagination, playing tricks on her in the stillness of the night. But as she tried to shake off the fear that had taken hold of her, she saw it again - a dark figure moving outside her window.

In a panic, she sprang out of bed and tiptoed to her grandparents' room, seeking refuge from the unknown. As she whispered her fears to her grandma, the old woman took her in her arms and held her close. Her grandmother's reassurances could not stop the terror that gripped Suzi's heart. As she listened intently for any sound outside, she heard a faint knock at the entrance door. Her grandfather, sensing the urgency in her voice, quickly rose to investigate. With bated breath, Suzi and her grandmother waited in the safety of the room, hoping that whoever was at the door would not harm them. The silence was deafening, broken only by the sound of her grandfather's footsteps as he made his way to the door.

She heard her grandpa's voice rising in anger and defiance, his words a fierce battle cry against the intruder who had dared to invade their home. She and her grandma walked into the entryway, their arms wrapped around each other in a tight embrace, their eyes wide with fear and confusion. At the dark entryway, a tall uniformed figure stood before them, his face hidden behind a black mask. He spoke in Serbian.

"What is he saying?" Grandma asked, her voice trembling.

"He wants us to leave the house and go with him right now," Suzi said, her own voice trembling with emotion.

"You can kill us right now, before I agree to leave my home," Grandpa declared, his voice ringing out like a battle cry.

"I'm not leaving my home!" he added, his defiance filling the room.

"Oh God," grandma said, her eyes flickering with fear. "Is he alone?"

"Yes," shouted Grandpa from the door, his words echoing off the walls.

"That's strange," said Grandma, her voice filled with confusion. "They usually come in groups."

"Come in, come in, young man," Grandpa called out in Serbian, his voice carrying an air of bravado. "I'm not scared of you. We are only two old people here with our granddaughter, and we won't go anywhere alive."

Suzi watched as the policeman straightened his gun. She could feel the fear coursing through her veins, and she knew that they were in grave danger.

"Please don't!" she screamed in Serbian, her words tumbling out in a desperate plea. "My mother is Serbian. We are peaceful. Please don't kill us. There's only us here. Please don't!"

But the policeman was unmoved. He held his automatic rifle aloft, with a grim determination in his posture.

"Get dressed and come with me right now!" he barked, his words ringing out like a death warrant. Suzi gasped. She recognized that voice. She thought she was delusional for a moment, but then it hit her like a bolt of lightning.

"Alex," she said, her voice shaking with disbelief. "Is that you?"

"Quick!" he said, his voice urgent. "I don't have time for chit-chat."

Her grandparents didn't seem to know what was going on, but Suzi knew. She hadn't seen her brother since that day when their mother left, but she recognized him now, even in his Serb police uniform. She walked closer to him, her heart pounding in her chest. "Grandpa, " she said gently in Albanian, looking at Alex and then grandpa, "This is Alex. Your grandson Aleksander. Leka..." she said like she was going to introduce them to each other. Both grandparents didn't move. They looked at Alex in his Serbian police uniform but said nothing. It was as if they were not surprised as much as Suzi was. She was stunned too, perhaps expecting them all to embrace each other. But Alex knew this was their grandparents house! Why did he cover his face with the mask and why didn't he speak in Albanian to their grandparent? How could he even point his gun to them? Suzi was all confused. "Let's go, please" Alex finally said in Albanian. "You have to come with me, away from the village, now!" Alex pleaded.

"I'm not going anywhere!" Grandpa declared again, his voice filled with a fierce determination. "You can go with your brother if you want to," he said quietly.

Suzi took a deep breath, her mind racing. She knew that her brother was determined to get her out of there. She didn't know why but she knew she had to trust him and go with him. But what about her grandparents? And so, she spoke the only words that she could think of. "Alex," she said, her voice firm and steady. "You don't have to do this. We can work something out. Please."

For a long moment, Alex said nothing. He stood there, his gun pointed to the floor.

"Fine," he said at last, his voice barely more than a whisper. "I can't force them to leave. But me and you, we have to go now. There's no time to waste. I'll explain things later."

Suzi felt a wave of relief wash over her. She didn't know what was going to happen next, but for the moment, at least, she felt safe going with her brother. She was going to be with him and that was all that mattered at the moment.

She rushed back to her room in a frenzy of emotions. Her heart was pounding, her thoughts racing, and her body trembling with anxiety. She had been searching and worrying about Alex for days, and now, finally, he was here. She had missed him.

"Come on!" Alex said, beckoning her with a frantic wave of his hand. "We have to go. Now!"

Suzi barely had time to grab her coat before Alex hustled her past their grandparents, who were now sitting quietly in the living room. She quickly went over to hug them and say goodbye. She shut the door behind her as she and Alex sprinted to the car.

"Get in!" Alex whispered, pushing her into the back seat. "And keep your head down." Suzi had so many questions, but she didn't dare ask. Alex was in a state of panic, his eyes darting back and forth, his hands gripping the steering wheel tightly. They were driving fast, too fast, through the village roads and then on the highway.

"Where are we going?" Suzi finally blurted out.

"Shh!" Alex hissed. "No talking. Just keep your head down and stay quiet."

Suzi tried to calm herself as they drove on, but her heart was pounding so hard she could barely breathe. Finally, they pulled over on the side of the highway at the edge of a mountain.

"I can't come with you," Alex said, turning to face her. "But you have to go. Take this flashlight and this money." He thrust a handful of bills into her hand. "Take that trail over there," he said, pointing the flashlight to a narrow path that wound its way through the forest. "And don't stop until you reach the village on the other side of the border."

Suzi was in shock. "What's going on?" she pleaded. "Please, Alex, tell me!"

"There's no time," Alex shouted at her. "Just go! Hurry!" He came out of the car and hugged her tight as Suzi stumbled out of the car. It looked like he was crying.

"Come with me! Don't leave me alone please! " Suzi begged him.

"I can't," he said "You go and don't stop. I'll come and get you when all this madness is over. You can do this! You have to do this! Promise me, you won't stop till you reach the village on the other side of the border."

"I promise," Suzi told him, reluctantly releasing him from her embrace.

Suzi ran up the trail as fast as she could. She was panting and sweating, her heart racing, as she climbed the steep hill. She was scared like she had never been scared before. The flashlight was too dim in her hand just enough to lighten the dirt road that she wasn't supposed to trail off of. "Just keep going" Alex had told her "and don't turn back under no circumstance". She walked and walked faster and faster focusing on the trail, ignoring the sounds of the forest. The sunlight was creeping up and she stopped a few times to gather her breath and wipe the sweat off her face.

When she reached the top of the mountain, she turned around and looked down at the valley far below.

She gasped in horror at the sight.

The whole valley was on fire, smoke billowing up into the sky. She could hear bombs exploding and gunfire echoing in the distance. She tried to look for her grandparents' house, but there was too much smoke and she was too far.

She thought of her grandfather's words from a few hours ago: "You can't take me out of here alive" Suzi broke down, her tears blurring her vision. How could this have happened? Why did they burn the village? All those people? The stench of the burning fields and the screams of animals were reaching all the way to the top.

She thought of Alex and his uniform. She didn't know what to think or what to do. "Keep walking and don't stop!" he had told her. There was no going back.

How could this have happened to those people? she questioned again in disbelief.

She thought of the sweet face of her grandma, the gentle hugs from her grandpa, and their happy smiles when they received her in their home a few days ago.

She thought of the neighbours that came to see her and brought her gifts. The girls her age that came to invite her to their house to make sure she wasn't feeling lonely. So many kind people in that village - what a tragedy. She couldn't even bear to imagine what was happening to them right now. Sitting atop the mountain, crying, sobbing for what seemed like a long time. She couldn't keep her eyes off of the village engulfed in smoke and fire. Eventually, she forced herself to get up and start walking again. Wiping away her tears, she turned her back on the horrific scene in the valley. She felt like a coward, a traitor for not running back all the way to help, or do something for her grandparents. But she had to keep moving, no matter what. She couldn't remember how many gruelling hours she had walked until she reached another village on the other side of the border in Albania.

———

She pushed away the memories of that horrible day of her life that left an eternal scar in her heart and stood up from her bed and made her way to her children's rooms. She felt grateful for the luxury of her large, beautiful house, nestled in the outskirts of Prishtina. The gated neighbourhoods that were built after the war and catered to the new wealthy elite, had become her refuge, and she revelled in the extravagance of her lifestyle. Her estranged husband, Bashkim, was a successful politician who had amassed a considerable fortune and Suzi had done the same in a surprisingly short period of time. She had no need for Bashkim's financial support or anything else from him for that matter, but he insisted on providing for his family, especially for their autistic son, Rron, who needed the best care possible.

Suzi had to admit that despite their differences, Bashkim was a good father.

She never asked him where the money came from, nor did she care. With so many other worries on her plate, the source of his wealth in a poverty-stricken country like Kosova was the least of her concerns. "The whole system is corrupt," Bashkim would often tell her. "You either play the game or you're out of the game completely. That's how the international community that helped liberate this country wants things here. They're Peace Cartels," he would say. But Suzi had no interest in his rhetoric.

"I don't need your money," she had told him repeatedly. "Just leave us alone." But deep down, she knew he would never do that.

As she went back to her bed, she was wide awake, unable to fall asleep. Memories of her high school days began to resurface, particularly her close circle of friends. Before the war, Suzi had been popular, never missing a single party or event. She was the life of the party back then, a popular figure that everyone seemed to know. But the war changed everything, tearing apart their world and scattering her friends across the globe. As she lay in bed, she couldn't help but ponder about the fate of many close friends who had disappeared from her life. Suzi lost touch with many of her friends and she often wondered about their fate. Had they been able to weather the storm of war, or had they been consumed by its cruel and unforgiving nature? How had they rebuilt their lives, if they had managed to survive? She had continued to be in touch with Ariana till recently. She couldn't even remember when they'd stopped seeing each other. Ariana's sudden avoidance of her puzzled Suzi. She remembered Ariana had begged her to give Bashkim another chance, a move that could have been orchestrated by Bashkim, Suzi thought, given that he and Ariana worked together in the same office. It made sense that Ariana would take Bashkim's side, as he was her boss, and Ariana was dependent on her job.

Despite her confusion as to why her friend would all of a sudden avoid her and not talk to her at all, Suzi empathised with Ariana especially because she felt for her struggles with mental health. It was ok with her if Ariana took the side of Bashkim. She understood and empathised with her even though she remained offended.

In retrospect, Suzi thought that she didn't really know much about Ariana on a personal level. They have been very close friends but somehow they have never talked about their personal struggles or inner thoughts. Perhaps it was the fear of innadvertently digging up painful memories of the past. No one wanted to be the friend responsible for triggering tears or dwelling on past sorrows, especially when their intentions for meeting and going out was to share laughter, drinks and good times in an effort to escape their daily struggles. Looking back, Suzi realised that Ariana was an icreadibly closed-off person, a true introvert who didn't talk much about herself. While Ariana was a good listener, Suzi recognised that over the years, Suzi knew only basic details about her friend. They had been there for each other, especially during those first years after the war, without needing to say much. They would often get together, listening to music, sharing laughter and tears, accompanied by bottles of beer or wine. Both understood that talking about the past would only ruin their evenings together so they avoided such discussions as much as they could. They understood each other better in silence and keeping conversations away from the subject of the past, and that was enough. They never once mentioned what had happened during the war.

———

Bashkim had met them both, Suzi and Ariana at the same time, in a caffe in the city, right after the war was over. Suzi remembered clearly that evening like it happened yesterday.

In a quaint cafe, illuminated by the flickering glow of generator powered lights, they sipped on their drinks and shared stories of their experiences during the war and their aspirations for the future. They spoke of foreign organisations that were hiring people, newspapers that reported on the situation in Kosovo, and the constant struggle for basic necessities like water and electricity. It was a time of uncertainty, as people sought to rebuild their lives and find a sense of normality in the middle of the chaos. Even during moments of despair, there were moments of happiness, as people sought out friendships and connections that would help them navigate the challenges that lay ahead. The thumping beat of the music filled the room, drowning out all other sound. The three of them leaned closer together, with muffled words and high spirits with the pulsing bass and pounding drums in the background. As the conversation flowed freely, Bashkim's past as a warrior was revealed. The girls, enthralled by his tales of battle and heroism, listened with rapt attention. And when he lifted his shirt to reveal the scar that bore witness to his battles, their breaths caught in their throats. Ariana, unable to watch, turned her head away and closed her eyes, while Suzi reached out tentatively and traced the outline of his scar with her fingers. In that moment, she was overcome with a sense of awe, a deep admiration for the man who had faced the horrors of war and emerged triumphant. A man who didn't abandon people in their time of need, unlike how she felt she had, but instead stood up and offered assistance any way he could.

As the night wore on, Suzi found herself falling under Bashkim's spell, drawn to him by a mixture of his bravery and the intensity of his presence. She got starstruck and a love was born out of admiration and respect for a hero who sat before her. Their conversation drifted towards the future and their deepest desires. Ariana's conversation came out as harsh and angry. She spoke of her adamant refusal to ever marry or bear children, and she spoke of her burning hatred for army uniforms, regardless of who wore them. The weight of her words settled heavily on the minds of Bashkim and Suzi that became uncomfortable at times. Suzi couldn't help but reflect on that evening, years later, whether Ariana's words had been the deciding factor that led Bashkim to choose her over Ariana as his romantic partner. She also wondered if Ariana had sensed her immediate attraction to Bashkim and deliberately claimed disinterest in serious relationships to encourage his attention toward Suzi instead. Suzi knew that Bashkim held a strong affection for Ariana, and their bond was somehow different from the one she shared with him. However, this had never bothered her, and she maintained her friendship with Ariana over the years. Even Suzi's children had grown fond of Ariana and she had been a presence in their lives, all these years. She held the role of a godmother to their son. But now, Suzi was certain that Ariana had sided with Bashkim after their breakup.

As the conversation had unfolded in that small cafe during their first meeting, each of them, including Suzi, revealed things about themselves that left Bashkim visibly surprised. Suzi shared about her family's magnificent house, a piece of prime real estate, that had been inherited by her after the tragic events that befell her family. Suzi's father had built that house from scratch but they had never been able to inhabit the house due to the interruption caused by war. Now that grand house sat empty in one of the finest neighbourhoods', solely in her posesions. Suzi confessed that she didn't know how to go about selling or renting it. With the influx of the foreign embassies and international organisations seeking office space in the area, it presented a good opportunity for her but she felt overwhelmed by the complexities of navigating through the paperwork required to rent or sell it. No doubt she could use some help. And who better to help her than a war hero and a rising star in their new country's politics stage. Bashkim had seemed very impressed with her dilemmas. He had generously offered to help Suzi in any way he could. Upon understanding whose daughter Suzi was, he had respectfully offered her his deepest condolences, acknowledging the honour and bravery of Suzi's father who had staunchly refused to participate in the crimes committed against his people.

"He was a true hero, and a man to be respected," Bashkim said, his voice resonating with reverence. Suzi's eyes had misted over with gratitude, her voice breaking as she thanked him for his words. "My father refused to be complicit in the atrocities that were being committed against our people, he refused orders of the party and so he chose to end his own life." She had explained the situation of her father further to him. "Knowing that someone like you, a war hero that fought the people that drove my father to death, and who gives him the respect that he deserves, means a lot to me." she had told him.

The memory of her father, an Albanian politician who had dedicated his life to building an ideal socialist society, weighed heavily on Suzi's mind. Despite the slanderous whispers that had started to circulate around his name because he had been a part of what was a dreaded Yugoslav Government in Kosovo, Suzi remained fiercely proud of him. Her father, like many of his generation, had been a staunch believer in Yugoslavia's socialist vision, a vision that had promised brotherhood and unity amongst all nations within its borders. He had devoted his life to creating a better world for the working class, and his passion had always filled Suzi with a deep sense of pride. But now, after the brutal fall of Yugoslavia and when the ideals of socialism had disappeared, so too had the legacy of her father. People spoke ill of him and of other Albanian politicians who had served under Yugoslavia. But for Suzi, her father's memory remained untarnished. She remembered the fire in his eyes, the unshakable belief that he had held in a better tomorrow. "His disappointment when he saw the complete destruction of his beliefs and ideals was something that he couldn't take anymore," Suzi had said, her voice filled with bittersweet ache. How can one give up on ideals that were taught to him all his life? He was made to believe that Yugoslavia was the perfect society of equal citizens where Albanians, Serbs, Croats, Bosnians, etc - all of them dedicated themselves to built this brotherhood and unity.

Her father's ideals, along with those of many others from his generation, were ruined by nationalism and hate culminating in a brutal war he could have never have foreseen. Was it her father's fault for being too idealistic? Perhaps, but Suzi remained faithful to her belief that those ideals were fundamentally good and progressive, and that it was nationalism, from all sides, that ultimately led to their demise. On the contrary, Bashkim argued that such ideals were unattainable, given the lack of democracy and the historical oppression of smaller nations like the Albanians by stronger ones within the Union. "Besides," he added, "Albanians were unnaturally paired with Slavs and arbitrarily divided into numerous countries." Suzi preferred not to delve into complexities of politics. To her, people were either good or bad and she knew her father to be a good man who never caused harm to anyone. This understanding was reinforced by Bashkim's words of praise for her father.

Suzi knew that her father was liked in the society despite his position in the previous establishment and she believed that his connections to the old political elite would come in handy even after the war. So when the opportunity presented itself, she wasted no time in utilising them to her advantage. With the help of her family friends, Suzi was able to rent out her large house to a Western embassy that was looking to establish a presence in Prishtina. The rental income that she received exceeded her expectations, and within a short span of time, Suzi found herself transformed into a wealthy woman.

Looking back on that night when she and Ariana first met Bashkim, Suzi couldn't shake off the feeling that Bashkim had been attracted to her for all the wrong reasons. She now suspected that he was nothing more than an opportunist who had used their relationship to climb the social ladder and accumulate his own wealth with the help of hers. Rumours of his infidelity over the years only fueled her anger as she found herself increasingly isolated and alone in her marriage. Eventually, Suzi made the difficult choice to end the relationship weighed down by the concern of her children's well being, particularly Rron. Though she and Bashkim had shared years of love and had built a good life together, there was this constant bitterness that had eroded their bond over the years. Their marriage had run its course and at the end, there was no anger left. They were both resigned to its conclusion.

———

As the night grew late, exhaustion began to wash over Suzi. She stifled a yawn, her eyes lingering on the flickering lights of the outdoor lawn coming through her large bedroom balcony window. She knew that it was time to retire for the night, but first she had to make sure that everything in the house was in order and secure. She couldn't help this sense that someone was watching her and her house at all times.

Suzi's feet padded softly across the hardwood floors as she made her way to the front door. She checked the locks and the security alarm, ensuring that her home was safe and secure. Satisfied that everything was as it should be, she moved on to her son's bedroom checking on him once again. As she pushed the door open, a warm glow spilled out from the hallway, illuminating her son's peaceful features. She stood there for a moment, taking in the sight of him, feeling her heart swell with love and tenderness. She would do anything for him, anything to ensure that he would have a good life despite the challenges brought on by his autism. Suzi's eyes filled with tears as she thought about all the hardships that her son faced as he grew up and all the obstacles that he would continue to face in the future. But she was determined to be there for him, to support him, and to love him unconditionally. And as she closed the door to his room and made her way to her own bed, she knew that she would never give up on him like she felt that her mother did on her, no matter what the future held.

Four

FATIME

As Fatime lay in her bed, quiet and motionless, she assumed the position she had perfected over the years - her hands delicately folded beneath her cheek, her body scooped to one side. Through the years she had learned how to control the urge to move or toss and turn in the bed. Despite the aches that had become all too familiar from the never-ending work around the house and the strain of keeping still for hours, she remained steadfast in her resolve to resist the urge to move.

The tension in her body was a constant presence, a knot that refused to unravel.

Even though her eyes remained closed, she couldn't sleep. She repeated prayers in a soft murmur, the words an endless stream of comfort and hope, whispered into the dark. "Bismi Allah al Rahman al Rahim..." she intoned, over and over again, as if the repetition would somehow bring the peace she craved. Her lips moved softly, forming the sacred words with reverence and devotion. She prayed for rest, for tranquillity, for the chance to escape the unrelenting ache that had taken up residence in her body. In the stillness of the night, her whispered prayers were a lullaby, a soothing balm for her weary soul. She lay there, suspended in the space between wakefulness and dream, her body aching and her thoughts scattered in a relentless whirlwind of worries. The only sound that broke the silence was the steady rhythm of Agim's breathing who, as usual, lay on his mattress on the floor, on the other side of their bed. His sleep now punctuated by the occasional snore, a recent addition to the symphony of sounds that he made in his sleep and that accompanied their nights. It had been so long since he had slept beside her on the bed that she had almost forgotten the warmth of his body next to hers, the softness of his breath on her cheek. She longed to hold him close, to offer him comfort and solace in his moments of distress. But he remained resolutely distant, a solitary figure on his mattress on the floor.

She had begged him to join her in bed, especially on the nights when he was plagued by nightmares. She had watched helplessly as he cried out in his sleep, his distress a palpable presence in the room. Her heart ached for him, broken every time he woke up in tears or screamed in terror. He would not let her touch him, would not allow her to hold him close. Even in the grip of his most harrowing nightmares, he kept his distance, crying silently as she looked on, unable to offer the comfort he so desperately needed. And so she lay there, listening to the sound of his breathing, her heart heavy with the weight of all that remained unsaid between them. Whenever she looked at him, she could see the pain on his face, a constant presence that never seemed to go away. She felt his pain in her bones, and this sorrow that weighed heavily on his heart was her constant worry. She wanted to help him, to ease his burden, but he refused her every effort.

They hardly spoke now, their conversations reduced to brief exchanges in front of his mother or others, a facade of civility that masked the gulf that had opened between them. She longed for the days when they could talk for hours, lost in the easy flow of conversation, but those days seemed distant memories now. He carried his pain like a burden, his eyes betraying the secrets he kept locked deep inside. She could sense the weight of his anguish, the scars left by his time in jail, but he never spoke of what had happened to him there. She knew that his pain was a private thing, something he had to bear alone, but it broke her heart to see him suffer in silence. And so, she watched him from afar, a silent witness to his struggle, aching to help him in any way she could.

Fatime cursed that cold Monday morning of December 1999, a few months before the war. As that cold December morning dawned, Fatime had felt the chill of the impending winter seep into her bones. The political situation in Kosovo was tense for years now, and no one knew how it was going to end. She had thought that she and Agim were making the best they could out of the situation and that they would be fine.

She remembered the time when they fell in love. She had been a star mathematician, with a gleaming collection of trophies and accolades that spoke volumes of her smartness and skills. Her diplomas and school awards were an endless source of pride displayed in carefully chosen frames all over the house by her parents for all the guests to see.

In contrast, Agim was the quiet history buff, a self-proclaimed nerd who shied away from the limelight, yet who possessed a charm that drew people towards him like a magnet. It was during one of the school's events for star students in their third year of High School that they found themselves smiling gleefully at each other, blushing and giggling without regard for anyone else in the room. It had been a dance night and they were both dressed in their best clothes, smelling of fresh soap and she was wearing lipstick for the first time in her life. It was a bright red lipstick that her mother had made her put on and it brought out the whiteness of her beautiful teeth. Her profoundly black eyes seemed to have absorbed all the light of the room and now that light was dancing on her eyes' surface creating a mesmerising effect for which she was not aware of at all. All her deep intelligence was hidden inside those eyes leaving a lasting impression on Agim who couldn't take his eyes off of her that night. As they swayed to the rhythm of the music, she had been swept away by his deft movements, his charm, and the effortless way in which the two of them seemed to connect. That night, they had fallen in love, their hearts beating as one.

As the months passed, their love deepened, and their bond grew stronger. The memory of that first dance remained in her heart, a reminder of the magical moment when their lives had intertwined, and a love story had begun to unfold.

They got married after High School closed just before their graduation as things were getting worse in the country. It was both their parents that encouraged them to move in and live with each other, because "you never know what is going to happen. "At least you'll be together and not continue to meet out of the house all the time" they had said. It was dangerous to meet and venture out of the house because of the heavy police presence in the streets. Their young marriage, that was only a mere agreement between them and their families and it didn't involve any signing of marriage certificates or anything like that. They didn't even have a party. This didn't bother them one bit, instead their union was imbued with a fervent passion that mirrored the honeymoon phase. Fatime counted her lucky stars for having found Agim, not just as a loving partner, but also as a true friend. His warm heart and kindness felt like a gentle protection from the world, and she reciprocated his love with equal passion. Their shared experiences at school, a familiar group of teachers and friends, and a mutual neighbourhood ensured that their conversations never ran dry. Though the world outside was gloomy, they were blessed with a thriving business that defied the odds. Schools and university suddenly closed to Albanians, factories were closed to them too and no Albanians were allowed to hold any government jobs. Everyone seemed to be out of work, but they had managed to carve out a living that was beyond survival thanks to Agim's parents. The supermarket was a godsend, a rare glimmer of hope so every day, as she navigated the narrow aisles, scanning shelves and scribbling notes, she felt grateful for the support of Agim's parents. They owned a supermarket on the ground floor of their home and every aspect of their livelihood was sustained by Agim's parents, who had sacrificed everything to ensure their only son's prosperity. From food to clothing, furniture to bills, nothing was left to chance. The small supermarket that they opened for Agim and her to work in, was an anchor of stability and the apartment on the second floor of their big house was a nice place to live. She and Agim had been happy that amidst the chaos, they had found anchorage in each other, and they had the love and support of their parents.

The day that Agim was arrested by the police, played often in her head as a day that she, Agim and their life changed forever. As the sun rose on that frigid December morning, she finished cleaning up the remnants of their breakfast, the clink of dishes echoing in the empty kitchen. With a sense of urgency, she wanted to hurry to the supermarket where her husband, Agim, awaited her help with sorting through stacks of paperwork. She was a whiz with numbers and she handled all the accounting for their small business. Just as she was about to finish her chores in the kitchen, she heard a brawl out on their street, right in front of their house. She heard loud arguing and she wondered who would be causing trouble so early in the morning?

She quickly went outside on the balcony to see what was going on.

The sound of shouting and scuffling grew louder, sending shivers down her spine.

Her heart started racing as she looked down on the street below in front of their supermarket. What she saw there left her reeling, her world turned upside down in an instant. Policemen were dragging Agim out of their shop, their harsh words and cruel actions leaving her feeling helpless and afraid. She had rushed out to intervene, their neighbours looking on in stunned silence from the safety of their balconies. Desperate to help Agim, Fatime could only watch in horror as he was beaten mercilessly by the police. Her heart was pounding in her chest as she tried to make sense of the chaos unfolding before her eyes. She cried out, her voice trembling with fear and anger, but it was too late. Agim was gone, taken away in the police car. In that moment, Fatime felt as though her world had come crashing down around her. She was numb, her mind struggling to comprehend the enormity of what had just happened. The shock and fear had left her paralyzed, her heart torn from her chest and taken away with Agim. For in that one terrible moment, she knew that life as she knew it would never be the same again.

For six long weeks, Fatime and Agim's parents had waited to hear what had happened to him and were very worried, their hearts heavy with the weight of uncertainty. They had exhausted all avenues of inquiry, leaving no stone unturned in their desperate search for answers. They had gone to the police station, hoping to find someone who could shed some light on Agim's whereabouts. But all their efforts had been in vain, as they were met with hostility and contempt. The political situation in the country had reached a boiling point, with tensions running high and the threat of violence looming over everyone's heads. People were being arrested and detained without any justification. Albanians had no protection anymore. Fatime often found herself wondering what they could have done differently, how they could have avoided this terrible fate. She now blamed herself and her loved ones for not recognizing the danger that lay ahead.

As the days turned into weeks, Agim's fate remained shrouded in mystery. People offered their speculations, their theories, their worst fears. Maybe he had been sent to fight in Bosnia. Maybe he was languishing in some Serbian jail. Maybe, they whispered, he was already dead.

Fatime couldn't accept any of these possibilities. It didn't make sense. What reason could there possibly be for Agim's disappearance? He was a simple shopkeeper, a kind and generous young man who never harmed anyone. Perhaps he had refused to give the police a bribe, or maybe he had stood up for his rights in some way. But even that seemed unlikely. Agim was too smart to provoke the authorities, too aware of the risks. In her heart, Fatime knew that something terrible had happened to Agim but without any proof, without any leads, she was left with nothing but her despair. She prayed for a miracle, for some sign of hope, but the days continued to pass, bleak and empty. As the country continued to spiral into chaos, Fatime struggled to make sense of it all. What kind of world was this, where innocent people were snatched away from their homes without any explanation or any warning? How could she carry on, knowing that Agim was out there somewhere, suffering, or worse? She didn't know if he would ever be back and if she would ever see him again. What was she going to do without him? Her life at their home; Agim's parent's house, now seemed like an intrusion without him by her side and she didn't know how to behave. In his absence, the home they shared no longer felt like hers. Questions and dilemmas consumed her thoughts and she was beside herself, unable to eat or sleep for weeks. It was at that time that she had realised how important her economic independence would be. Perhaps if she had gotten a diploma in accounting, she wouldn't have felt so utterly dependent on Agim and his family. It was just a fleeting thought at that time, one she couldn't have imagined would shape her perspective in the years to come.

Six weeks had passed before out of nowhere, Agim appeared in front of his shop on a quiet Sunday morning, a mere shadow of his former self. Fatime and Agim's parents had rushed to embrace him, tears streaming down their faces in disbelief that he was alive. He was frail and broken, his eyes betraying the horrors he had lived. His body was a mass of bruises and wounds, and Fatime took it upon herself to nurse him back to health. She was grateful he was back home. She was terrified that he would suddenly fall ill and die that she even watched over him at night. She fed him, washed him and tended to his wounds with the gentlest of touches. He slept for days on end and was unable to walk without her support.

After months of nursing him with the greatest care, his body healed but his soul remained wounded forever. Like a broken vase that can't ever be glued back together again, his broken spirit was never the same again. The man who had come back to her was a stranger, his eyes haunted. Fatime looked at him, the man who had been her lover, her friend, and felt a deep sense of loss because she didn't know who he was anymore.

He lay down in the same room as her now, but he might as well have been in another continent. They were two people who had once been so close, now strangers to each other. Fatime wanted to reach out to him, to bridge the distance that had grown between them, but she failed at every attempt. He had closed himself in an impenetrable shell and didn't let her in. All she could do was watch him, her heart aching with the knowledge that he was lost to her forever. His once outgoing personality had been replaced with a quiet, angry person that wanted to be left alone at all times. He barely spoke and avoided contact with anyone, including Fatime. Despite her best efforts, he remained distant and uncommunicative. The only time she saw any sign of life in him was when he started praying - something he now did regularly, five times a day, every day. In a desperate attempt to connect with him again, Fatime began praying too, hoping that through prayer, they would find their broken connection again. As time went by, Fatime watched in despair as her husband slipped further away from her.

He grew a beard and started dressing differently, spending his days at the mosque.

He told her to cover herself with a hijab, a garment she had never worn before and made her know that she had no choice in considering other options. She didn't even know anyone who wore the hijab, not even his mom or other elderly women. Agim himself had brought the scarfs and other garments for her from the mosque. It was a shock that she didn't know how to explain. She could have never imagined herself wearing such a foreign garment. At first, it felt like she was wearing a costume, like she was trying to become someone else. But she complied, hoping that it would help her husband find the peace and happiness he desperately needed. She was willing to do whatever it took to bring back the Agim she once knew, hoping he would appreciate her efforts and talk to her and love her again.

But her efforts were in vain;gone was the cheerful friend, the talkative, happy man who looked forward to spending time with her every hour of the day. He had been replaced by a stranger who seemed lost in prayer and meditation. All these years she had longed for the man she had married, but he never reemerged. She could not comprehend these profound changes in him after his captivity and she never found out what had happened to him in prison, after all these years.

———

Fatime's lips moved silently in prayer but her mind was preoccupied with thoughts of tomorrow, thoughts that had consumed her for weeks. She rehearsed her plan for the hundredth time, her heart heavy with doubt one moment and then alight with hope the next. The weight of guilt lay heavy on her shoulders as she contemplated what she was about to do. She was going to finally do something that would forever alter the course of her life. She couldn't even say the words: divorce, escape from, leave, her husband. These words sometimes seemed treacherous and made her feel awful and guilty. In the depths of her heart, she trembled from the mere thought of being branded a traitor, an outcast among her people, a woman stripped of virtue. She was aware that the force of condemnation against her would be ruthless. She understood that she would be labelled with all kinds of vile titles, reserved for women that didn't conform to the rules of religion. Within the confines of this small tight-knit community in this part of the town, transformed into a devoted haven of religious people after the war, she will transform into a figure of shame—a scary legend and a cautionary tale to be told to little innocent girls of how they should never behave. Fatime knew her escape would become a tale of caution to young girls that were trapped by the clutches of a traumatic post war-ravaged world where religious extremism found fertile ground; a grim warning of what they must never succumb to.

In the quiet corners of her fragile soul, she clung to the fragments of her true self, desperately yearning to be understood. The judgments to be cast upon her were nothing more than misguided whispers carried on the winds of ignorance, she thought.

Even if her spirit trembled at the thought of this undeserved fate, she resolved again and again to endure and go through with her plan. She hoped she had the strength to remain steadfast in her truth, for in the depths of her being, she knew her innocence shone brighter than the fires of condemnation. As she thought more about her life with Agim, the difficulties of their marriage and her patience all these years, anger seared through her, a flame fuelled by the knowledge that she should have taken this step years ago, when youth and vitality were on her side. She told the part of herself that was feeling guilty that she had nothing left to lose.

No one cared if she stayed or left. Her husband would simply pray harder, while his mother would relish the opportunity to find a new bride for her son, a woman who could provide her with the grandchildren she so desperately desired. For years, Fatime had believed that it was her duty as a wife to remain by Agim's side, to tend to his needs and the needs of his mother. It took her years to realise that they had simply allowed her to stay out of pity, viewing her as a hapless creature in need of their mercy. The realisation cut deep, and with it came the knowledge that her marriage, once a bastion of love and devotion, had long since withered and died. Now she knew that she could no longer remain in this loveless marriage. The future was uncertain, but the weight of the past was too much to bear. Her prayers had given her the courage to take the first step, to leave behind the only life she had ever known, and to venture into the unknown.

She had listened to her mother-in-law chatter away on the phone, bad mouthing her all these years while Fatime's heart had sunk every time she heard what was being said, making her feel helpless. The older woman always spoke of women who could be potential new brides for Agim, listing their virtues and qualifications, as if they were nothing more than a line-up of candidates vying for a job. She had mentioned a widow, a woman who had lost her husband in the war, or another one, who clung to the hope that her lover would return from abroad to sweep her off her feet, but never did. It seemed there were endless possibilities for Agim to find himself a new wife. Her mother-in-law's lamentations filled the air of their home, the weight of her sorrow was very palpable. "He could have had three or four children by now," she sighed. It was a familiar refrain, one that she repeated daily, as if to remind Fatime of her shortcomings. When her mother-in-law confronted her, urging her to step aside and make way for a new bride, Fatime remained silent. It was the custom to defer to one's elders, to show respect even in the face of such a callous insult. But inside, she seethed with anger, her heart heavy with unspoken words. She longed to tell her mother-in-law the truth, to scream that it takes two to make a child, that Agim's depression and illness were not simply the result of her supposed barrenness. She yearned to call her out on her ignorance, to ask why she had not spoken to her son about these matters instead of confronting her. But she remained silent, her thoughts locked away in the prison of tradition and expectation. In the silence of her mind, Fatime screamed in frustration, a desperate cry to escape the clutches of her mother-in-law's expectations. What did the old woman want from her? To find a new bride for Agim and then step aside, as if she were some sort of puppet with no will of her own? To play the role of the dutiful mother-in-law to her husband's new bride? Even the thought of it was all too much to bear. But she knew better than to speak her mind to her mother-in-law. The old woman had an answer for every question. She often recounted tales of unnamed souls who had effortlessly found contentment in their marriage through mystical means. It seemed that within her repertoire, there always existed a story of a "certain" woman, seeking help from a clairvoyant or a revered cleric, their pleas answered, and wombs blessed with the miracle of life. In her eyes, Fatime was dismissed as obstinate and faithless, a defiant soul unwilling to surrender to such notions. It was as if her mother-in-law lived in a world of her own, where her words were law, and everyone else's feelings didn't matter. And so, Fatime stayed silent, her eyes fixed on the ground, hiding her anger and hurt. She wanted to protect not only herself, but Agim as well, shielding him from his mother's expectations and hiding his secret from his mother. No one, not even his own mother, knew about the torture and trauma he had endured during those six weeks in jail but Fatime heard his moans of pain and saw his tears in the darkness of night. As she listened to her mother-in-law's demands, Fatime couldn't help but wonder: did the old woman truly care for Agim, or was she only concerned with fulfilling her own desires? It was a question that haunted her, even as she kept her thoughts to herself and prayed for the strength to endure.

As warm tears trailed down her cheeks, Fatime was still struggling with a daunting decision: to leave tomorrow and never return, or to stay and endure the endless suffering. Could she bring herself to abandon Agim, leaving him to his own devices? Would she regret it for the rest of her life? Or would he be better off without her, relieved to not have her around? She was infuriated by this weakness crawling in on her every few minutes. For years, she had held out hope that he would change, that he would heal. She begged him to open up to her, to share his feelings with her, but all she received in return was anger and aggression. She longed for the effortless bond they shared as school friends, when they would do anything to help each other. But now, he was distant and unapproachable.

"I can't go on like this," she whispered to herself in between prayer recitals.

"I'm drained." she told God.

Her mind drifted in the hope of seeing her mother the next day. She missed her. She yearned for the safety and comfort of her childhood home, where she could find the strength to make the tough decisions ahead.

She told Agim this morning before he went to the mosque that she had to go and see her mother who wasn't feeling well. He didn't say anything, just nodded in agreement so she had her duffle bag all ready for tomorrow. She couldn't wait for the night to end and for her departure to finally come.

FIVE

BESA

Besa's mother had always been interested in her daughter's appearance. It was a part of their Albanian culture, her mother had said, to take pride in one's appearance and to always look their best. As Besa sat in the living room, her mother asked if she had made an appointment for her hair for the party later that night. Besa shook her head, admitting she didn't know where to go. "Leave it to me," her mother said, a smile spreading across her face. "There's a new hair salon just down the road, next to the supermarket. I'll call them now." Besa smiled at her mother's enthusiasm. Regardless of the distance between them, her mother always found a way to remind her to take care of her beauty routine. Even through video calls, she would comment on Besa's appearance, urging her to put makeup on or get her hair done. "Albanian mothers are tough to please," Besa would often joke with her American friends. "They want their children to be the best in the world."

Besa felt a twinge of disappointment when her mother criticised the dress she had carefully chosen for the reunion party. It was a festive black dress, with a unique cut and an intricate design that she had paid a fortune for. But her mother was unimpressed, and Besa felt a bit frustrated. She realised that not having a mother close by to criticise her about every decision in her life, had acually been a good thing.

"There are much better dresses here," her mother exclaimed, surveying Besa's wardrobe with a critical eye. "You're coming from America, and you will wear this simple dress? It looks like an office dress, not a party dress."

"Mom," Besa protested, her voice rising in frustration. "I'm not 18. This is a very expensive designer dress, and I'm wearing it."

"But it's black," her mother objected. "No one wears a black simple dress at a reunion party." Besa sighed, knowing that arguing with her mother was pointless. She looked at the dress again, wondering if she should change into something else, but ultimately decided to wear it. She knew she looked and felt comfortable in it, and that was all that mattered.

Besa sat down at the small kitchen table and savoured the delicious roasted peppers with cream, relishing in the familiar taste of home. She kissed her mother's hand once again, feeling grateful for her mother's hospitality and kindness. She was finally surrounded by the comforting smells of Albanian cuisine yet she couldn't help but feel a pang of sadness as she remembered her father, who had passed away after the war. Despite the distance and time that had passed, her mother still made her feel like a child, spoiling her with her favourite foods and showering her with love.

Besa knew she would never take these moments for granted, especially after longing for them for so long. She will cherish each and every one of them. And as she looked at her mother's smiling face, she felt a sense of contentment and belonging, knowing that she was exactly where she was meant to be.

Besa still remembered the sound of her father's weak voice as he spoke those last words to her on the phone.

"I want you to be happy," he had whispered, his voice barely audible.

"Promise me, whatever happens, you will hold on to happiness!"

"I promise,". Besa had replied , holding the phone tightly to her ear.

"I promise," she had repeated several times, ensuring her father heard her clearly. Since Kosovo had always been in a political turmoil, it seemed not just her parents, but all adults sympathised with the younger generation. They were constantly worried over their mental well-being, feeling powerless to guide them towards a better future and a life filled with optimism and joy.

Her father's sudden passing had left her feeling empty and lost even though they lived miles apart. The abruptness of his death, without any warning, shook her. She longed to be home, surrounded by loved ones, to properly mourn his loss. But in a foreign land where she didn't know many people, she struggled to find consolation.

As a child, she had never grasped the significance of her grandfather's often repeated saying: "Death is closer to an older person than the shirt they're wearing." Now, reflecting on those words, she finally understood their profound truth. Death could strike at any moment, regardless of time or place. In the end, what truly mattered to the elderly was having their family by their side to bid farewell as they departed from this world. Yet, she hadn't been there for her father and she knew the weight of that regret would linger for as long as she lived.

Despite the ache in her heart, Besa held on to the memory of her father's last words to her lovingly. She had promised him that she would stay happy and optimistic, no matter what challenges she faced. And though it was a difficult promise to keep, she tried her best to honour it.

Whenever loneliness threatened to engulf her, she would embrace herself, remembering her father's comforting words. "Whenever you miss me, hug yourself because I'll be right there in your heart, always," so that's what she did knowing that he would forever reside within her, a constant presence in her heart.

———

After her mother arranged an appointment at the hair salon, Besa rushed to get there and get ready for the evening festivities of the Reunion. As she settled into the chair of the salon, she felt a little nervous watching the young hairdresser fussing with her tools. She had always been particular about her hair, preferring a natural look that reflected her inner spirit rather than the stiff, over-styled hairdos that seemed to be the trend. Glancing around the salon trying to see if by chance she recognised anyone, she felt a sense of foreignness wash over her. Aware that the women around her could easily identify her as an outsider, she felt a subtle sadness of alienation. She remembered how in the past she too was able to identify people that came from abroad to Kosovo for their summer vacation. At that time the number of people living in the diaspora had been very small compared to now. In this tight-knit community everyone knew each other intimately or through a family member or friend. They usually knew where everyone in that neighbourhood lived, who their friends and family members were. After two decades away, she now felt as an outsider but she could still guess the conversations the women would have about her the moment she would step out of the salon. They would speculate about her success abroad based on her appearence- the style of her clothes, the intricacy of her hair and makeup. Her fashion choices would be scrutinised, with particular attention paid to her shoes, purse and jewellery.

With quiet politeness, Besa requested that her hair not be overly styled, no fancy bun or puffed coiffure, and certainly no excessive use of hairspray. The hairdresser seemed taken aback, as though insulted by Besa's simple request for a natural look.

"But you're going to a party," the young woman insisted, her voice laced with annoyance. "Surely you want to look special?"

Besa shook her head firmly, her gentle demeanour contradicting her insistence.

"No, no," she replied firmly. "Just a normal blow-dry but not too straight. Maybe a bit of a wave, that's all."

The hairdresser sighed, clearly irritated by Besa's lack of enthusiasm for her skills. It was as if she was desperate to showcase her talent and win the admiration of her client, perhaps even capturing the perfect before-and-after shot to share with her social media followers. But Besa remained determined in her request, refusing to compromise. For her, true beauty went beyond mere outward appearance, including fancy makeup and hairstyles. She had encountered too many seemingly beautiful individuals whose inner ugliness overshadowed their looks, reinforcing her belief in the importance of inner goodness. She knew that her choice to embrace her authenticity would make her shine far brighter than any fancy hairdo ever could.

She looked at herself in the mirror, her dark blonde hair falling on her shoulders with a natural curve, her brown large eyes encircled by delicate wrinkles, deep with wisdom and life experience gathered through her life. Already relying on reading glasses, she found a certain charm in this sign of ageing. Time had flown by quickly, she thought, studying her reflection in the salon's mirror. Though twenty years have passed since she last was in this neighbourhood, the younger self still glanced back at her from the mirror. The sights and sounds of these familiar streets flooded back still vivid in her mind's eye. She remembered how at 19, two days before being expelled from this neighbourhood and becoming a refugee , her mother had cut her hair short in a desperate attempt to make her look like a child. Besa didn't know at the time but her mother had hoped that if they came face to face with police or paramilitaries, making her daughter look less appealing to them in any way, would probably save her life. Besa had cried as her chestnut locks had fallen into the bathroom floor while her mother had tried to assure her that this was for her own good and that her hair would grow back in no time. The inherent beauty of innocence in the young people though, was a quality that transcended the mere outward appearance and the will of evil to destroy that innocence was greater.

As the hairdresser went to work, deftly wielding her tools with precision and care, Besa knew that she was in good hands. For even if the aim was to only have a simple blow-dry, she could see the true artistry and skill that went into every stroke of the brush, every spritz of hairspray. She took a moment to enjoy the beauty of the salon, marvelling at the skill and care that went into each detail. Everywhere she looked, there were happy, cheerful customers, chatting amiably as they waited for their turn in the stylist's chair. Her thoughts drifted to her mother's words that she told her this morning about the aftermath of the war and how, in the wake of so much devastation and loss, people had become almost desperate in their desire for joy and celebration. They sought to reclaim their lives with a fervour that bordered on desperation, eager to make up for the lost years and to rediscover the simple pleasures of everyday existence, she told her. And for many, this newly found sense of urgency manifested itself in a renewed focus on their appearance. Where once pride had been enough, now there was a deeper need to project an image of happiness, of success, of prosperity. For some, it was a matter of regaining their dignity in the wake of loss and upheaval. For others, it was a means of achieving a new social status, of climbing the ladder of success through sheer force of will. And for some others, it was a way to gain the attention and admiration from people that they so craved. In short, the people of this city were in a hurry to look pretty, to look happy, to look rich.

As Besa observed the women around her, she couldn't help but be struck by the sense of friendship that filled the salon. It dawned on her that coming to a salon wasn't just about the beauty treatments, rather it was about the conversation, the connection and the shared experience of transformation that truly defined the atmosphere. The women chatted eagerly with the hairdressers, who were generous with compliments and quick with advice. They exchanged stories, gossiped about mutual acquaintances, and laughed easily. Even the most reserved of them seemed to loosen up in the warmth of the atmosphere. The salon visits were more like therapy sessions than anything else, she thought. Sitting beside her, two young women were deep in conversation, eagerly discussing the upcoming weddings and festivities that awaited them. They spoke with excitement in their voices, describing their chosen outfits in vivid detail and hoping that their hair would match their overall look. They sought out each other's advice and suggestions, delighting in the prospect of looking their best.

Besa watched with a smile, feeling a sense of kinship with these women. There was something magical about the energy of the salon, a sense of joy and lightness that was infectious. With a sudden determination, she turned to the hairdresser and told her: "You know what?", her voice clear and firm. "I want to have my hair coloured and highlighted before the blow-dry. And can you do my makeup too?"

The hairdresser's smile was one of approval, and Besa felt a surge of excitement.

This was it. This was the transformation she needed.

The experience was nothing short of magical. As the hairdresser worked her magic, Besa felt invigorated. Her hair came alive with colour and texture, shimmering in the light. And as the hairdresser finished with a flourish, applying the perfect makeup to accentuate Besa's features, she knew that she looked and felt her absolute best.

With a newfound sense of confidence, Besa left the salon, ready to take on the city of her youth once more, after twenty years absence. The magic of the salon had worked its wonders, and she felt renewed, reinvigorated, and ready to face the evening ahead.

———

April, 1999

James, a dedicated worker for the UNHCR, looked at the exhausted Besa with concern on his face. She had just arrived in the camp with a group of thousands of other people from Kosovo. She was pale like a ghost and was shivering violently. She received first aid, and was given an IV. Her mother had changed her wet socks and tried to find a blanket to cover her. "Are you feeling better?" James inquired gently, after the IV was finally done. The tent that they were in was huge and it reminded Besa of a circus tent, but this one was white and plain and not colourful like the one of a circus that came to Prishtina during summers when she was a child.

"I'm very, very tired," Besa replied, surprising him with her perfect command of the English language. As he took in her weary expression, James noticed the growing number of people outside the tent, all of them seeking urgent help. A growing crowd trudged towards the camp, their spirits crushed by the unfathomable horrors that had befallen them. Mothers, with tear-streaked faces, clutched their children tightly, their eyes haunted by the terrors they had witnessed. For many, this was the furthest they had ever been from their humble homes, the violence they had endured unimaginable. As far as the eye could see, the crowds of displaced humanity stretched out in a never-ending sea of lost souls. More arrived by the minute, on foot or by bus, their identities stripped away as they were herded towards the camp. Exhausted, afraid, and uncertain, they were faceless in the eyes of the world, reduced to mere statistics in the annals of history. In the wake of their sudden displacement, the once-resilient individuals appeared stunned, shattered by the realisation of how easily they had been transformed into helpless creatures, stripped of their autonomy and reduced to the pursuit of basic necessities. Desperate for a roof over their heads, they scoured the surroundings for any semblance of shelter, hoping to find respite from the cold. Even the most basic of human needs, such as the privacy of a toilet, had been snatched away, leaving them feeling vulnerable and exposed. It was a stark reminder of how quickly one's life could be uprooted; how fragile human life truly was.

A young mother sat opposite Besa on the makeshift ambulance tent. With her few days old baby in her arms, tears were streaming down her face as she tried to explain the infant's incessant crying. Besa, feeling better compared to the frail young mother, quickly conveyed the mother's distress to James and his two colleagues, pleading with them to help her. "The baby is so small and refuses to latch," the mother wailed, her anxiety palpable. She was trying to explain to James and his two colleagues that her baby had been crying non-stop for almost two days, since they had to flee their house and were forced to leave and cross the border on foot to try and survive the murdering spree of the army that had destroyed their village. It was clear that the young mother was on the verge of a breakdown. James and his colleagues were doing their best to help her and her baby, and they were grateful for Besa's assistance in translating her plight. "Thank you for translating. That's a big help," James acknowledged, his gratitude evident. Realising the importance of Besa's contribution, James made a request of her: "Could you please come back as soon as you feel a bit better and continue translating for us? As you can see, we are overwhelmed, and your help would be invaluable."

Without hesitation, Besa agreed, promising to return in just a couple of hours. And true to her word, she did, her tireless efforts making a significant impact on the camp's desperate situation. Besa couldn't bear to sit idly in the cramped tent, her heart heavy with the sight of the massive misery unfolding before her eyes. The handful of people desperately trying to help was simply not enough to alleviate the crushing weight of despair that loomed over the camp. The cold and damp tent where her parents lay covered with heavy military blankets was suffocating, filled to the brim with bodies in various states of distress. She knew she had to do something, anything, to help them. Still weak and emotionally frail, Besa made her way to meet James. "I want to help any way I can," she declared, her voice resolute. She was worried about her parents, whose older bodies had borne the brunt of the traumatic days they had endured. They were among the many elderly people that the trauma of the last few days had taken its toll on. Their spirits had been shattered, as if slowly succumbing to a death by a thousand cuts, as they bore witness to their country and homes being consumed by an unforgiving force beyond their control. The destruction was beyond anything they could have ever imagined, and it seemed as if they were dying of broken hearts, unable to comprehend the enormity of the devastation wrought upon their lives. Besa couldn't bear the pain and sorrow etched into her parents' weary faces, and her heart ached for the loss they had suffered.

She felt a surge of responsibility, as if she were now the adult tasked with caring for her once vibrant parents, now rendered helpless like children amidst the chaos of the camp. Besa tried to take charge now; "Focus on saving them! Focus on saving them!" she whispered to herself. A mantra to anchor her amidst the multitude of worries and uncertainties swirling around her. When she got the opportunity, she talked to James hoping he could help her and her parents to get out of the camp. She was determined to get them out of that miserable place. With different policemen now patrolling the camp, denying exit to anyone and even organising the relocation of refugees to other locations or countries, the task became increasingly complex. Families risked being torn apart if they weren't cautious in advocating for their own well beign. "My father is very sick. We need to reach a hospital in town." she begged him for a solution. "We have family and friends in Skopje that will take us in. We just need to leave this camp. I fear my parents won't survive in these conditions." She spoke urgently, condensing her plea into a few concise words, hoping to convey the severity of their situation and grab Jame's attention. With so many people in need, she understood that the UN workers, including James, couldn't help everyone to get out of there. It was impossible. She had to use this opportunity with the connection she had forged by assisting them with translation.

With a worried look on his face, James promised to do everything in his power to help. "Let me see what I can do," he said, his voice steady and reassuring. "There has to be a way for ill people to get the full care that they need out of the camp. Our sources are limited here and we have to find an option."

Grateful , Besa pleaded with him again and again to find a way to help her parents, her eyes shining with a mixture of hope and desperation. "Please!" she implored, speaking from the depths of her heart.

As the night descended upon the camp, so did the chill that

crept into Besa's father's frail body. He grew progressively worse as the hours ticked by.

When the first rays of daylight finally broke through the darkness, Besa and her mother knew they had to act quickly. They carried her father to the emergency tent. Thanks to James' tireless efforts, they were soon on their way to a hospital in Skopje, the capital city of North Macedonia and later that night to her father's good friend's house in the Albanian part of town. Besa made a promise to return to the camp and help translate and she did. Now as a UN staff member, she worked all day at the camp and stayed with her parents in the evening. Feeling fortunate, Besa found a little hope amidst the hopeless situation of being a refugee. Everything was horrible but they survived and now she would work and earn some money so she and her parents could survive. She believed that the liberation of Kosova would arrive soon, and they would go back home. She missed home so much already.

As the days stretched on and the weight of the work grew heavier, Besa found herself struggling to keep up. The emotional toll of so many sad stories and laments weighed heavily on her, and her mental state began to suffer. She wasn't sure if she was strong enough to continue hearing and translating all those horrors for much longer. She found herself overwhelmed, her emotions spilling over as she struggled to translate the harrowing stories of those affected by the tragedy. She started to doubt that she was truly capable of shouldering this responsibility. James intervened again and helped her once more to clear her head. "You're doing a great job," he told her, his words a balm to her frayed nerves. "But you must learn to set aside your emotions, to wipe away the tears and focus on the essence of what we're doing here." He spoke of the enormity of their task, of the difference they were making in the lives of these people, and of the immense satisfaction that came with knowing that they were doing something truly meaningful. "Can you try to see your job from that point of view?" he asked, his voice gentle but insistent.

She considered his words, turning them over in her mind, and slowly but surely, a sense of purpose began to take root within her. Yes, the work was difficult, but it was also vital, a lifeline for those who had lost everything. She thought of the women, the children, the elderly, all of them struggling to survive in the wake of disaster, and she knew that she couldn't turn her back on them.

Besa had always prided herself on her ability to anticipate the unexpected, to stay one step ahead of the curve. She was a mature person for her age who realised now that she knew how to adapt and thrive in even the most challenging circumstances.

But there was one thing that she never saw coming, one twist of fate that caught her completely off guard.

Reflecting on it now, she could hardly believe how it had happened - the unexpected feelings of love in the circumstances that she was in. In a strange environment of the refugee camp, a sense of routine gradually settled in after a few days. Children engaged in soccer games with international troops, mothers found creative ways to entertain their children and distract them from the misery, and people gathered in circles and talked for hours. Day in and day out, Besa and James worked side by side, tirelessly assisting its inhabitants in the emergency tent. Tears were shed frequently, but in this midst of sorrow there were occasional moments of laughter, gossip, and shared cigarettes and beverages. But love was the last thing on anyone's mind.

It was a typical day at work when the realisation struck Besa. It was like a puzzle piece falling into place, revealing the whole picture. She didn't know what love was or how it felt but she knew one thing - that she thoroughly enjoyed James's company. As they worked together on this particular day, assisting an injured child, a new UN worker who had recently arrived at the camp, approached them with a question that would shift Besa's perspective on her friendship with James. "Are you two a couple?" the newcomer asked, her eyes bright with curiosity. Besa and James exchanged surprised glances, momentarily taken aback by the unexpected inquiry. "No," they replied in unison, their smiles masking the sudden flutter of their hearts.

The young woman shrugged; her demeanour was nonchalant. "You just seem like you are," she said, "and there's nothing wrong with that." Besa felt her cheeks flush with embarrassment, her mind racing with conflicting emotions. How could this stranger see something that she herself had been blind to all along?

That evening, as Besa lay on the makeshift mattress in her father's friend's house in Skopje, doubts and insecurities flooded her mind, threatening to overwhelm her grasp on reality. The misery of the situation was overwhelming, suffocating, and it seemed impossible that she would find herself falling in love or even thinking about it. It felt embarrassing to say the least. Her thoughts spiralled with questions and self-doubt. Had she acted inappropriately with James? Had she inadvertently conveyed the wrong impression? What would he think of her now? Was it possible to fall in love amidst so much pain and suffering or was her mind playing tricks on her? Tears welled up in her eyes and she didn't really know what to do. The thought of just not showing up for work at the camp ever again, crossed her mind. But wouldn't that be even more embarrassing and immature? What would her colleagues think? They would undoubtedly come looking for her. What explanation would she offer? Her dilemma seemed unresolvable.

After hours of agonising tossing and turning, Besa decided to bury her feelings and just carry on as if nothing had changed between her and James, because in reality nothing did. Slowly, she sat up and looked around the room, taking in the quiet darkness surrounding her. Her parents snored softly in their bed above her head, oblivious to the turmoil that churned within her. She felt a sense of urgency growing within her and couldn't wait for the morning. She thought how James would only feel sorry for her in case she had somehow given the impression that she was in love with him.

The following day, she woke up with heaviness in her heart, feeling as though her spirit had been drained. She didn't bother much with her appearance, throwing on a pair of jeans and UN t-shirt before heading outside to wait for the car. As she caught a glimpse of the approaching vehicle, her heart began racing erratically, beating faster and faster with each passing moment. A bright smile lit up her face, perhaps a touch too eagerly. However, she quickly realised that others were also in the car with James, which made her feel more uncomfortable. She muttered a soft hello and quickly made her way into the car without giving James a second glance. Sensing something amiss, James turned to her with concern on his face. "Is everything alright? You look exhausted. Perhaps you should have taken a day off," he suggested gently. As they began their journey to work, she found herself lost in her thoughts, not paying much attention to the others or engaging in conversation. She only released exasperated sighs that escaped her lips, as she berated herself for being so foolish. The weight of her own self-doubt and insecurity had taken hold, leaving her feeling awkward and embarrassed. Was it wrong that she could even think of love under those circumstances? Why did she find herself eagerly anticipating every opportunity to be near James?

Besa's heart raced as she navigated through the camp, her mind consumed by thoughts of James. She knew she needed to speak to him, to clarify the situation.

As she walked throughout the camp, talking to people, checking on the needy, she found herself replaying in her head every interaction she's shared with James in her mind. Was it her unconscious mind that painted James as her saviour, a foreign knight in shining armour that came to rescue her and her people? How can a girl resist falling in love with a knight, a saviour? Yes that must be it, she concluded.

As she approached James' tent, Besa felt her heart pounding in her chest. She could hear voices inside, and her stomach turned with nervous anticipation. Taking a deep breath, she stepped inside. After she got a chance to speak privately to James, she launched into an apology, telling him how much she admired his work and how sorry she was if she had given him the wrong impression. James listened patiently, his expression softening as she spoke. This was not the time to get into these conversations, he told her gently. An old man, laying in the makeshift bed was shivering. He was trying to explain to James how he had had stomach pain all night. His face was covered in sweat. Besa started translating right away. She felt stupid about what her mind had been occupied with all that time.

———

As Besa looked back on her past, she still had a sense of disappointment in herself that she had refrained from seeking her parents advice on this matter until the very last moment, during those difficult times. She had believed herself to be strong and mature enough to manage her emotions independently. Moreover, she had convinced herself that her parents wouldn't comprehend her worries and didn't want to burden them with what she deemed irrelevant, even embarrassing problems. Now, in hindsight, she recognised her naivete. Despite her extensive reading, viewing and memorization of literature, films, poetry and songs, nothing could have prepared her for the emotional turmoil wrought by the combination of war and love. These two forces, stark contrasts in their own right, had a profound and overwhelming influence on her state of mind. At the tender age of 19, she found herself navigating through these tumultuous feelings, stumbling and making mistakes along the way.

That evening after a gruelling day's work, James shared uplifting news that lifted her spirits. "I heard that everything is coming to an end soon! NATO is entering Kosovo, and the Serb forces are leaving as we speak." The words sounded almost unbelievable. A surge of joy swept through the crowd, mingling tears with laughter, disbelief with overwhelming happiness. In that moment, she was overcome with more emotions, tears streaming down her face once again. In that atmosphere of celebration, James had wrapped his arms around her, holding her close and told her that he loved her. She never forgot that moment of pure double joy, it stayed engraved in her memory forever.

———

"Promise me you will come back!" Her father's words had echoed in her mind, haunting her year after year with their poignant plea. She could still feel the loving clasp of his hand on hers as he signed as a witness to her marriage certificate, a union with James. But her father's request had not been a one-time occurrence; rather, it had been a persistent and fervent plea that he repeated to her for several days in a row, after she announced her intention to leave for the United States with James. For Albanians, a promise -called Besa just like her name - was not to be taken lightly. It was a sacred thing that her very name represented, embodying the highest echelon of human dignity and character that had endured through centuries. Countless legends and songs had spoken of the sanctity of Besa - the Promise - as a given word that held far more weight than a mere vow. Through the ages, people had risked everything, from their lives to their families and livelihoods, to uphold their Besa - Promise, Oath.

And so, she had promised her father again, her voice firm and unwavering, as she boarded the plane and left her weeping parents behind at the departure gate in Skopje airport, that she would come back. But as she journeyed to her new life, her heart ached with the knowledge that her father's plea would linger with her, a reminder of the immense weight that lay behind even the smallest of promises let alone a big promise like the one she gave to her father. She thought about the promise she had made to her father every day since she'd moved to the US even though he never mentioned it again in their weekly phone conversations. He must have realised that that was too much that he asked of her.

It had been hard for Besa to get adapted to her life in the US. She found herself adrift in the sea of unfamiliarity. Like every other immigrant, she went through a phase of a tremendous culture shock. The sheer magnitude of the cities and the country as a whole made her anxious and feeling so small in the vastness of things. Her country that she left behind felt to be in a different world, a memory from a different realm of the universe and here she felt like she was dissolving into insignificance against the backdrop of this country's vastness. She didn't know anyone here except James whom she had met in a completely different environment. She felt lost for years but then somehow liberated as she got used to the country and the mentality. She realised that in the US, she could be the person that she wanted to be and she could do the things that she always wanted to do. There was a boundless potential to shape herself anew. It was a revelation.

The 'Country of Birth?", a simple question on an Immigration form, had thrown her into confusion. She had turned to James, seeking guidance. "What should I write?" she had asked him, her voice tinged with uncertainty.

"Kosovo," James had replied without hesitation.

She had been hesitant. "Will they know where it is?" she asked.

"Write Former Yugoslavia, too, just in case," James had advised.

The question of 'Ethnic Origin' had been easier for her to answer. With determined strokes, she had written "Albanian" on the application form. Yet, as she looked at the document, she still was afraid that people here just had no idea where her country was and that she would remain an enigma and her request for citizenship unanswered. Whenever the question of her origin arose, especially when meeting with Jame's friends and family, she felt herself transported back to the labyrinthine streets of Prishtina and her parents' apartment. She had trouble explaining to these free individuals who cherished their individual uniquness and watched her with pittying, sympathetic eyes, the high importance that people in her country gave to being part of a nation, to belonging and preserving a national identity. She wanted to tell them that she hailed from a country where happiness and suffering walked hand in hand, where the struggle to preserve one's identity was not merely a choice but an expected rite of passage passed down from generation to generation. Living in a crossroads of ideologies, of countries, of empires, her people had learned to live with a quiet acceptance of their circumstances. They had fought to preserve their culture, their language and their way of life since times unknown and now they were free.

Of course she didn't say all those things to James's friends and family. She told them about all the hardships of her war ravaged country, with people that are truly grateful to the United States for enabling their freedom and their return to the country after the horrors of war were stopped by Nato forces.

She thought of James often in the past few days since she arrived in Kosovo. She found that the physical distance has altered her perspective on some things and transformed the perception subtly, as she found herself now observing her city and her country through the lens of an outsider for the first time. She found herself trying to envisage her homeland through James's eyes, and a sense of detachment started to linger in her. She wouldn't admit to anyone, especially not to her mother, that she too, at least for a few moments at a time, viewed her country through the prisms of Jame's gaze, as an outsider.

———

Years went by and James got busy. His patience waned by the weight of Besa'a constant yearning for acceptance or understanding. He got bored with the tales of her childhood and her friends and family. With passage of time, he stopped noticing how clean she kept the house and the novelty of the home cooked dishes ceased to impress him. He started to be late for dinner, to get held up at work and to not mind going out without her. It took time for her to realise that she should find the courage to start taking care of herself and become independent. As James told her many times: she was smart, she was capable and she should go out there and make her dreams come true. Up until then, she thought that in marriage her dreams should only be ones concerning their household and him. She wanted to get pregnant and have a family first but that didn't happen. Being a wife, mother and having a career was surprisingly very hard in the US and even if she got pregnant, pursuing other things in life was nearly impossible in the US.

After getting her Green Card, she embarked on a journey that would change her life once more. She had always envisioned herself - a well-educated, independent woman because that's how she was raised. She had always nurtured within herself that vision and she set up to work finally on her ambitions and to get a University Degree. In her family getting into higher education had been an unnegotiable endeavour. So when she entered the halls of NYU, she felt that she finally found a place where she belonged.

She couldn't pinpoint exactly the time when she and James had stopped talking. It was a gradual progression when they simply didn't have anything to say to each other anymore.

Her father's words had echoed in her mind throughout her years at the University, a constant reminder of the promise she had made and gave her a purpose. To finish her education and go back home as she promised. And yet, year after year, she had found reasons to postpone her return to her homeland. She became engrossed in the opportunities and experiences that this new world offered her. Years flew by in what seemed a whirlwind of ups and downs. Meeting new people and learning new things kept her going as she learned to blend in what was her new home and her new country. She grew quieter through the years and almost invisible to people around her. She didn't speak much and continued to study hard. During her studies, she worked at an Albanian owned restaurant in New York City and shared a small apartment in Queens with an elderly woman who became like a second mother to her. She considered herself lucky again. She made it in the US with hard work and lots of determination. Her graduation day was one of the happiest days of her life. All her colleagues from the restaurant were there to congratulate her. Even James showed up with flowers and a friendly card.

Her father's voice may have faded from this world, but the memory of his words and the weight of his love remained with her, guiding her on this journey back home. It was a journey that held both sorrow and joy, both fear and hope, as she finally fulfilled the promise she had made. In her mind's eye, she imagined her father looking down upon her, witnessing her return and fulfilling the promise that she had made. Despite a profound sense of satisfaction at the thought of her father smiling in heaven and being proud of her for returning, a lingering sense of unease gnawed at her. The homecoming that she had so eagerly anticipated was not as fulfilling as she had imagined. Instead, she found herself transported to a time long gone, a disorienting and unsettling experience that left her feeling adrift.

As Besa gazed pensively out of the window of her room every night since her return, her mind enveloped in a dreamlike haze, the world outside that window appeared both familiar and foreign. It was as if she had awoken from a twenty-year sleep, emerging from an alternative reality that had existed only in her dreams. The events of her recurring nightmare lingered in her memory, haunting her with their vividness and immediacy, while the life she had lived elsewhere felt like a distant fabrication, leading her to this moment suspended between past and future, with nothing in between. Besa's life had come full circle, offering her a chance to pick up where she had left off two decades earlier, but as a fundamentally different person. Despite her intimate knowledge of the city's streets, corners, and buildings, little had remained unchanged on the surface. She felt like an outsider in her own hometown, a stranger in a place she once called home. Every step she took was a journey of rediscovery, a testament to the person she had become and the life she had lived in the interim.

SIX

ARIANA

March, 1999

At nearly 19 years old, her heart swelled with love for Arben. She finally found the courage to confide in her mother about the relationship, only to receive a stern warning: "Don't tell your father." But she knew that her mother's words carried a deeper message, one that spoke to the generational divide between them. "You're too young," her mother said, her voice tinged with regret. "You need to go to university and create a path for yourself, unlike me. I had no choice but to marry after just one date with your father. I was so young." "Many are deceived into believing they're in love, only to realise later that their partner isn't what they envisioned," her mother continued solemnly. "That's why you must wait and don't tell your father. Once you publicly announce your relationship, it becomes official, and your choice of life partner is sealed. There's no turning back. You'll be committed to marrying him."

Her mother's own experience with love and marriage coloured her view of the world, imbuing it with a sense of caution and apprehension. "Thank God your father is a good man. I was lucky," she said wistfully. "So many of my friends weren't."

At that moment, her mother's words served as a warning, a cautionary tale of the perils of love and the uncertain paths it could lead into. She was urging Ariana to tread carefully, to guard her heart and not be swayed by fleeting emotions but Ariana's heart was ablaze with the flames of love for Arben. She couldn't bear to think of a future where she and Arben were not together, where their love had dwindled and waned. In fact, she wanted to marry Arben as soon as they were old enough, to spend every moment of their lives entwined in a love that knew no bounds. She refused to entertain the notion that Arben might not be the man she hoped him to be, that their love might not withstand the test of time. For Ariana, their bond was unbreakable, fortified by the two years of being best friends and kindred spirits. Their love for each other was pure, unadulterated, and unyielding, an unshakable force that defied all odds. They might have been too young to understand the complexities of love, but they couldn't help it. The love that they shared was instinctive, a primal force that propelled them towards each other, bringing them ever closer with each passing moment.

In Ariana's eyes, Arben was her soulmate, her other half, the missing piece that completed her. She was sure that their love was unique, especially because it happened at such a young age, a testament to the power of true love and the unbreakable bond that could be forged between two young, innocent hearts.

Romeo and Juliette only with a happy ending. Ariana vowed to cherish and protect their love, to nurture it like a delicate flower, and to hold onto it with every fibre of her being. Her mother was too tough on her, she thought. The weight of cultural expectations bore down heavily upon her, like a suffocating blanket that threatened to smother her individuality and crush her spirit. Her mother had instilled in her the virtues of obedience, respect, and good manners, insisting that these qualities were the hallmarks of a good Albanian girl. Ariana had conformed to the rigid expectations placed upon her till now, striving to be the epitome of what a young woman should be. Her mother had drilled into her the importance of "honour" and "saving face" that were so important within the Albanian community and society, emphasising how a girl's behaviour, her choices, her body, and her desires were all inextricably linked to these values.

The weight of expectation bore down heavily upon young women in Albanian society, burdening them with the responsibility of upholding the honour and reputation of their families. Ariana felt the injustice of this burden acutely, wondering why it fell so heavily upon the shoulders of women. Yet, as she looked around at the society in which she lived, she realised that this unfairness had become the norm, deeply ingrained in the cultural fabric of her community. The psychological impact of this burden was immense, exerting a powerful force that kept women firmly in their place. The fear of being shamed or accused of doing something shameful was ever-present, a constant reminder of the narrow confines within which women were expected to live their lives. From a young age, Ariana had been taught to fear the word "marre" (shame), understanding implicitly that it represented a threat to her reputation, her family's honour, and her very identity as a good girl. Anything deemed "shameful" - whether it be a simple mistake or a more serious transgression - was enough to trigger the powerful forces of shame and ostracism within her community. The list of shameful behaviours for young girls was a long and daunting one, encompassing everything from the mundane to the most serious transgressions. A girl could incur shame simply by sleeping in too late, failing to help with the chores, or talking back to an elder. Even talking too loudly could be seen as a breach of decorum, inviting disapproving glances and whispers from those around her.

But it was the more serious transgressions that struck fear into the hearts of young women, the ones that threatened to upend their lives and destroy their reputations. Wearing mini skirts or too much makeup, being seen in the company of boys too frequently, staying out late in the evenings or lingering too long in cafes - all of these could invite harsh judgement and ostracism. And then there were the most shameful offences of all, the ones that had the potential to bring immediate shame and disgrace upon both the girl and her family. Having a boyfriend and engaging in premarital sex were perhaps the most egregious sins of all, carrying with them the potential for devastating consequences. The greatest shame a young woman could bring upon herself and her family was to engage in premarital sex, an offence so severe that it could bring ruin to her reputation and the honor of her entire family.

In the eyes of society, the blame and shame fell solely upon the female, while the male partner in the act was absolved of any wrongdoing. It was a cruel and unfair double standard, one that perpetuated the idea that women were the guardians of morality and virtue, while men were free to indulge their desires without consequence. The burden of responsibility fell squarely upon the young woman's shoulders, who was expected to be vigilant and cautious in her interactions with boys, to avoid being lured into temptation by their sweet words and false promises.

The fear of shame and ostracism was a constant baton hanging over in the head of young women, a reminder that their choices and actions could have far-reaching consequences. And while some may have bristled against these restrictive expectations, for many it was simply the way things were, a reality to be endured and navigated with caution and care.

This, Ariana thought, was a frustrating predicament and she didn't comprehend why girls and boys weren't treated equally. The notion that her body was not solely her own, but rather a product of social constructs dictating how she should behave solely based on her gender, unsettled her deeply. The idea that her worth as a human being was tied to conforming to specific gender roles was profoundly unsettling to her.

The pressure to maintain her virginity, and the harsh consequences of failure at it, loomed over her like a dark cloud. It seemed unjust that a young woman's worth should be determined by her sexual "purity", while the men involved faced no such scrutiny or condemnation. In the end, Ariana realised that the social structures governing her body and her choices were far more complex than she had ever imagined, and that challenging them would require great courage and determination.

As Ariana listened to her mother's words, she felt a sense of confinement settling in her chest. The idea that life had a predetermined pattern, a set of rules that one must follow, made her feel trapped. She yearned for something more, something that went beyond just good grades and finding a good job and a good husband.

But her mother's words echoed the values of their society, where conformity was praised, while having a strong sense of individuality was frowned upon, even suppressed. The path to happiness was paved with caution and practicality, leaving no room for spontaneity or passion. For young girls like Ariana, the list of expectations were daunting. They were expected to be the perfect daughters, obedient and respectful, following the strict guidelines set by their parents and society. And while arranged marriages were no longer the norm, the pressure to conform to their parents' wishes in choices for their partner was still how things were done. Their approval or disapproval of their choice of a life partner could make or break a relationship. A young love had the potential to end in a disturbing or tragic way or for some lucky ones flourish into a happy life. Ariana wondered if there was more to life than just following a predetermined path. She longed for the freedom to explore her own desires, to chase after her dreams and to find happiness in her own way and that was what she was doing, going out secretly with Arben but she was worried that things would go wrong. What if her father disapproved? What if his family disapproved of her? Ariana was hopeful and believed her parents were not like some other parents. She was looking forward to her future with Arben. The teenage Ariana believed that the course of her life was hers to chart, with no external forces capable of altering her fate. How naive that notion seemed to her now. But then again, it was that youthful naivety that had allowed her to fall deeply in love with Arben at such a young age. She felt like a rebel and she didn't care what anyone thought or had to say about that. For she had found her soulmate in him, and she was willing to break all the rules for him.

Even after all these years, the memory of Arben's smile still had the power to warm her heart. It was like a radiant beam of sunlight that enveloped her cold heart and body, a warmth that she craved like a flower in need of sunlight. The ache of missing him throbbed throughout every cell in her body, and she longed to feel his embrace once again.

———

The memory of that cold spring morning in 1999 remained engraved in her mind like a tumour, threatening to engulf her body every day. She remembered vividly how she had moved like a thief for days in her own home, carefully packing her duffle bag, writing a farewell note, and placing it on the hallway mirror. Every step was calculated to ensure that her family wouldn't be disturbed by her departure. Without making a sound, she had put her shoes on, opened the outside door of the apartment and then closed it slowly, so she wouldn't wake her sleeping parents and her siblings and had run down the stairs and off the building.

She had felt a twinge of guilt, leaving the door unlocked. They never left the door unlocked at night, especially lately when trouble was brewing everywhere due to political upheaval and uncertainty . Her Father made sure the door was locked every night before going to bed. She had hoped for the best and told herself that one of her parents would wake up and notice the opened door and lock it. Her father slept very little and checked the door very often. Lately he seemed more worried than usual and was in a bad mood often. He had lost his job at the factory just like all the other Albanians lost their jobs in every field, overnight and collectively. People were in shock. They couldn't believe this was possible. Schools and Universities closed to Albanians, newspapers in Albanian language were banned and the only TV station in Albanian language got raided, seized and closed by police, live on TV. The situation was deteriorating very fast and continued to get from bad to worse every day. After almost the entire population was made unemployed, people struggled to make a living and support their families. Amid the chaos that had enveloped their country, many felt that there was no other option but to leave. The situation was grim and unforgiving, leaving little room for hope or optimism. Her father, however, even in that situation had tried to cling to the belief that this was just a temporary bout of madness, a fleeting moment of insanity that would soon pass. He refused to give up on the hope that sanity would eventually prevail, and that things would eventually return to some semblance of normalcy. It was a belief that was shared by many, who simply couldn't fathom that this nightmare could drag on for as long as it did. Even fewer people thought that it would get worse, which it did, over the course of a few weeks. She didn't tell her parents that she was planning to run away with Arben. Together they had made the bold choice to run away from all the seething troubles in their hometown. Even when they wed in a hasty ceremony at the town hall on her eighteenth birthday, Ariana remained tight-lipped about their union. The only witnesses to their nuptials were Besa and one of Arben's close friends, who stood by as they sealed their love in a private exchange of vows. But the decision to withhold such momentous news from her parents was not made lightly. It weighed heavily on Ariana's heart, and a nagging sense of guilt and uncertainty overwhelmed both her and Arben. Despite the fear and uncertainty that awaited them in their journey, they believed it was better to keep her family out of the loop until they had reached safety. They were old enough to take care of themselves, they thought.

Ariana poured her heart and soul into a long letter, left behind for her parents to find. It detailed their plans and intentions, assuring them that they were capable of taking care of themselves and would soon be in a position to help financially. The letter was a testament to Ariana's resolve in her choices and her unshakeable belief in their abilities to find happiness and prosperity away from this country.

As she attached the letter to the frame of the mirror in the hallway, Ariana made a promise to call her parents as soon as they arrived in Skopje, hoping to ease their concerns. She was even sure they would arrive there, before her parents woke up. It was just about a two hour drive.

Ariana and Arben had decided to leave their country as husband and wife, a choice that made them feel more mature and honourable in the eyes of their parents. Ariana was confident that her father would not be sad or angry with her for running away with a husband rather than a mere boyfriend. Throughout her life, she had striven to make her father proud, even when going against his wishes. She had dated Arben secretly, though she was sure her father had found out. Yet he had never stopped her from going out or lectured her in any way. In his own way, he had shown her trust and faith that she would do what was right, for which she was deeply thankful. Ariana was resolute in her decision to remain 'chaste' until legally married to Arben; they would consummate their love in a faraway land! Although she knew little about the intricacies of sexual intimacy, she was determined to uphold her family's honour and make her father proud. For Ariana, her chastity was a symbol of her commitment to her family's values and traditions. She was willing to sacrifice the pleasures of the flesh for the sake of her father's approval and the preservation of her family's reputation. In this way, she hoped to prove to herself and those around her that she was a woman of integrity.

"Uhm,..." Ariana would murmur softly and shake her head in disbelief of her past innocence, the simplicity of her perceptions and the naivety that defined her and her friends at that time. She also felt fondness for that innocence and she wished that it had never been tarnished in such a brutal way.

The girl that she was; naive, innocent, young and cocooned in the world of youth, had died that early morning of spring 1999, on the side of a road, somewhere close to the border with North Macedonia! What was left was a shell, a shadow of that girl that now lived only in her memory. How could that innocent girl ever imagine what terrible things lay in wait for her and for her beautiful boyfriend? How could she have known that, that fateful morning, when she jumped into the car, that she and Arben would kiss for the last time?

That morning, Ariana's heart had pounded with feverish excitement that she had never experienced before. It was a kind of anticipation that filled her with hope and joy, like a hundred butterflies fluttering in her chest. She was going to be with Arben forever, and they were about to embark on a journey that would take them far, far away from the war-torn country they called home. Together, they had meticulously planned their escape, mapping out their route to the neighbouring Macedonia and beyond, dreaming of starting a new life in London or the US.

Their dreams and plans had felt like a fairy tale, woven together by the threads of hope and excitement. The future was a canvas waiting to be painted by them, a world waiting to be conquered by their love and ambition. They had dreamed for days on end about how their life would be, who'd they become, what jobs they would do, how their house would look, how many children they would have, what their names would be...

The mere thought of their life together had made their hearts soar with joy as they spent endless days planning, wishing, hoping. In those moments, life had seemed a happy, rosy place, promising and full of potential but all they had to do was leave Kosova. With Macedonia being just a couple of hours away, their escape plan had seemed easy and doable without much effort or risk. They felt invincible, as if nothing could stop them. Their love was a fortress, shielding them from the cruelty of the world around them. All they could see was a bright future ahead of them, free from the turmoil that had ravaged their homeland.

But the reality turned out to be very different to what they'd hoped or expected. Unbeknownst to them, police checkpoints had been multiplied and sprung up in every corner and junction of all the roads leading out of the country. The officers stationed there were not your typical traffic police; they were armed to the teeth. Ariana and Arben had been so blinded by their plans that they failed to take this into notice. They were consumed by an intense desire to escape the grim reality of their war-torn country, a place that simply did not align with the bright future they had envisaged for themselves. They yearned to flee not only for their own sake but also to help their families financially in the future because they were struggling under intense hardship. The prospect of leaving the country together as husband and wife seemed like the perfect solution to their problems. It promised a new beginning, a fresh start, and a chance to build the life they had dreamed of. Her friend Besa had warned her, and even begged her not to drive to the border just by themselves. Travelling in groups would be safer, she had said; but Ariana had dismissed her fears, believing they would be less likely to be stopped if they were alone, just the two of them.

"Wish us luck! We'll be In God's hands", she remembered saying to Besa the night before they ran away.

As things turned out, she would lose faith in God forever.

———

Ariana could still not understand how they had missed noticing the armed paramilitary patrolling on the side of the highway on that cold early Spring morning.

The sun had just begun to rise, painting the horizon in a pink glow. It was that time of the early hour when daylight was pushing the night away, the time when the sun was showing its head slowly, like a baby coming out of a womb. It was the time of day when no people should have been out on the road yet.

She remembered the jarring screech of tyres as Arben brought the car to a sudden halt, ordered by a person in uniform that came suddenly on the road. Other paramilitaries emerged like ghosts from the shadows, in their dark blue uniforms, their faces covered with balaclavas, weapons in hand. At first their presence was a blur, indistinct shadows in the dark moving in front of them.

In that fleeting instant it seemed to her that the sun stopped rising, and the dark was engulfing them once more.

Ever since, she often dreams that instead of stopping the car, Arben presses the accelerator and the car magically starts to fly like in a James Bond film. In that dream, she feels enormous relief as they fly towards the rising sun. They both smile and laugh and hold hands drifting into pink clouds that surround them. After the dream, she usually wakes up and sobs uncontrollably.

How could they have been so naive? So stupid! She often thinks, beating herself about it.

Despite many warnings from friends, they felt confident they would make it through the border. Ariana often pondered why she had been so unaware of the dangers on the road that day. Was it because she rarely paid attention to the news, like her father? Maybe her youthful naivety made her think the situation wasn't as dire as people said. Or perhaps her passionate love for Arben blinded her to the harsh realities around her. In her heart, she couldn't believe someone could be so cruel as to murder or torture a young couple just to prevent them from crossing the border for their honeymoon. Like most young people, they couldn't imagine any human being capable of the vile savagery that ensued after they stopped the car. Their minds couldn't fathom such brutality and barbarism from fellow humans.

Ariana had rehearsed the speech in Serbian countless times in her mind, ready to recite it flawlessly if they were to face any interrogation at the border. With passports and their marriage certificate in hand, she and Arben also wore their slim gold rings as a symbol of their love and commitment. Ariana believed that these objects, along with their innocent appearance, would be enough to convince the policemen that they were on a harmless journey. How could they possibly be considered dangerous, Ariana thought, when their only intention was to start a new life together?

They were only a few miles away from an imaginary line on the landscape beyond which her whole life would have been very different, where her whole existence on this planet would have been very different...

Arben quickly opened the car window on his side. He exchanged greetings in Serbian with the policeman whose gun was hanging on his shoulder. The policeman ordered Arben to show him their documents, which Ariana handed to him right away.

She still remembers how the policeman smiled sinisterly when he read their Albanian names on the documents. She and Arben sat still.

He ordered them to come out of the car, sniggering.

Other policemen were now approaching the car, looking at them with strange intensity. Arben gave her an encouraging smile and touched her hand gently while nodding to her in reassurance that everything would be fine.

They got out of the car slowly, each on their side. She was scared, but she still hoped that everything would be fine.

Till the very last minute.

The minute when she saw in disbelief Arben's body falling into the ground like a tall cut tree, blood coming out of his curls. She felt someone dragging her away from the car. She remembers being shocked to the core, unable to process the scene she just witnessed. She called Arben's name several times loudly, asking him to get up! .

Arbeennn , Arbeeeeen , çou (stand up!) Arbeeen , Arbeeen....

When she became aware of what was happening, she looked at the policemen with contempt that she didn't know could exist in her.

She started screaming like she never knew she could. She kicked and fought like a wounded animal, with all the force that she had, till she fainted.

———

She lit another cigarette, the memory of that day always weakening her limbs, making her stomach turn upside down and her whole body ache.

The helplessness she felt while being held captive, like a sheep waiting to be slaughtered, still ignites fury within her, burning her insides.

She can still feel the aching of her back from being pushed on the cold hard ground and she still feels the pain in her body that she had never known it was possible to endure. She remembers how her body had shut down - frozen and her mind created a sense of detachment from her body.

Her legs, her thighs, her stomach, they didn't feel like they belonged to her anymore. They were just pieces of flesh that didn't feel as part of her. She was transformed into a soul that had left the body and was looking at what was happening to her body from above. She didn't want to see so she kept her eyes shut as she lost complete control of her physical being.

Hands, lots of hands touching her, pulling her hair, blood running down the insides of her thighs. The scent of alcohol, cigarettes and the stench of bitter dirty mouths. The aroma of blood, semen and sweat mixed with the burnt smell of gun fire. She couldn't breathe in the thick, harrowing charged air with animalistic euphoria of predators tearing up a helpless, frightened prey.

This memory and the utter shock that she had felt that day revisited her often. Sometimes it came onto her unexpectedly,completely paralysing her body.

No matter how much she tried to push the memory away, it was there in the corner of her mind at all times, ready to become the epicentre of her very existence; Ready to kickstart a panic attack after all these years and to never let her have a single night of peaceful sleep.

She was haunted and tortured by the memories of those dark days. She constantly felt tired. Sometimes, she couldn't get out of bed for days when the memory of that day engulfed her.

———

How could she possibly attend the Reunion Party tomorrow, when every moment would be spent searching the sea of faces for a glimpse of Arben? Even now, with no evidence of his death or a body to mourn, she clung to the hope that he was still out there, maybe somewhere in Serbia. Perhaps he had been wounded but not killed, taken prisoner and unable to make his way back to her. In her darkest moments, she wondered if he had lost his memory due to his injuries, unable to remember the way home. It was a fanciful notion, one she knew deep down was unlikely to ever come true , yet, she allowed herself to indulge in it from time to time, just like Arben's mother did. Maybe, just maybe, one day he would remember and come back to her, and all would be alright with the world once again. She imagines sometimes how he just shows up at her door, with a bunch of flowers or a box of chocolates, or a wrapped book.... She didn't really know and neither did she care about what he'd be holding in hand; as long as he showed up. Her heart aches at the thought of him, memories flooding back like a torrential downpour. She pictures him standing at her doorstep, his gentle knock echoing, reverberating through the tiny hallway of her apartment. With trembling hands, she would turn the door knob, her heart pounding with anticipation and fear.

But as he would stand before her, she would hesitate. He would look so different now probably, so much older than when she last saw him. Would she even recognize him? However, she was sure she would immediately recognise his smile, regardless of how he may look now. In that moment, all the pain and fear she had held inside all these years, would melt away, and be replaced with love so intense that she would sob uncontrollably in his arms. He would tell her that everything would be okay, that it was all just a nightmare and it was finally over. And for a brief moment, while she imagined all this, she would forget about the world outside. Their happiness would last forever.

Her mind often wandered into this imagined scene, a bittersweet fantasy that brought her both comfort and despair. She longed to see him again, to hold him close and feel his warmth, but the reality of his disappearance from her life weighed heavy on her heart. She knew the odds were slim, that the chances of him miraculously returning to her were in the realm of quantum mechanics but still, she clung to hope.

———

As the cold night air cut through her in the windy balcony, Ariana's head throbbed with pain. The sounds of stray dogs barking in the distance brought her back to reality, reminding her of the world outside of her thoughts. She is still worried about tomorrow and the reunion party. She could easily tell Besa that she wasn't feeling well and skip it, but the thought of disappointing her friend was hard. After all, Besa had travelled all the way from the United States and they didn't see each other in such a long time. For people like Besa, who lived far away from Kosova, these gatherings were a precious opportunity to reconnect with old friends and reminisce about the past. She knew she couldn't let Besa down.

Besa remained one of the few friends, perhaps the only one with whom she remained a close relationship, even if it was mostly through social media or occasional texts. They still talked the same way they did when they were teenagers, as if no time had passed. When she spoke to Besa on the phone, it felt as if life were the same as when they were young. Besa was a reminder of the girl she once was, embodying the innocence and joy of her childhood days. Their friendship had stood the test of time, sharing a closeness similar to that of siblings, transcending time and distance with an unbreakable connection she believed would endure forever.

However, Ariana had always imagined that their friendship would remain long- distance. Now that Besa was here and planning to stay here forever, Ariana felt a bit anxious. Would their bond withstand the test of actual closeness?

The winds of change had swept through their generation, tossing everything and everyone in all kinds of directions. Some had moved on, leaving old friendships behind and forging new ones. Others had retreated into themselves, consumed by work, family and everyday problems. Many had moved away. Ariana knew that her friendship with Besa was natural and enduring, and she didn't have to worry about being close friends again, even though they were now grown-ups, different people from before the war. However, she wasn't sure if Besa would like her now as much as they had liked each other's company back then. Did Besa know about the rumours that swirled around her, like a storm cloud gathering on the horizon? Did she know about the dark days when Ariana had lost all hope, and had tried to end it all? These were secrets that Ariana had kept locked away deep within her heart, secrets that she had never shared with anyone. Even Besa remained unaware of the trials and tribulations that had marked her life.

To calm herself, Ariana reassured herself that everything would be fine and that she didn't need to worry about Besa judging her. Besa was her friend who knew her better than anyone else. Ariana felt confident she would find the courage to share her story with Besa, to lay bare her soul and unburden herself of the weight she had carried for so long. That was the only way they could be true friends again—no secrets. She felt happy and relieved at the thought of finally being able to share her pain with someone who genuinely cared for her. The pain and grief that consumed her were too great to bear alone.

Until now, sharing her tragedy with others had felt like walking naked down the streets, exposing her wounds for everyone to see, something she wasn't ready to do. Yet she yearned to scream about the injustice of it all, to cry out for the world to hear, to shout from the rooftops that what had happened to her was a crime and that she needed justice to move forward with her life. She wanted to go on TV and talk about it, to write a book, to cry with her friends and Bashkim, to appeal to international organisations to jail the perpetrators of crimes against her, Arben, her family, and all the others who had suffered. But she felt too weak to do that. The word "shame" still held her captive, a dark and insidious force that bound her in silence and solitude. Now she was looking forward to seeing Besa tomorrow night.

She went back to contemplating what to wear at the reunion party. The Red Dress, a gift from Bashkim, seemed to wave to her from the depths of her closet. She knew that it would turn heads, make a statement, and draw all eyes to her. But was it appropriate? Was it too bold, too daring for the occasion?

Sighing, she gave up on the idea of finding the perfect outfit and retreated to the sanctuary of her bedroom. There, nestled among the pillows and blankets, she found solace in the presence of her furry companion, Mic. The soft warmth of his body and the steady rhythm of his breath calmed her nerves and eased her worries, allowing her to finally drift off into a peaceful sleep.

———

Ariana groggily stirred from her sleep, Mic meowing impatiently beside her. As she reached for her phone, the familiar sound of Bashkim's voice filled her ears.

"Hey sleepyhead," he greeted her. "I called you ten times already."

Ariana couldn't help but smile at the playful teasing in his tone. "Well, you finally woke me up. Happy now?" she told him, smiling.

Bashkim chuckled. "Are you going to the party tonight?"

"I don't know," Ariana replied, her voice growing serious. "I'm not really in the mood for crowds."

"You should go," Bashkim urged. "Go have fun!"

Ariana sighed, feeling torn. "I don't know...I'm not sure what to wear."

Bashkim laughed. "Wear the red dress for me, please."

Ariana hesitated, unsure if she was ready for such a bold statement. "Hmm...that dress might be too much."

"No, it's not," Bashkim reassured her. "You look beautiful in it."

Ariana's eyes filled with tears at his words, her doubts and fears melting away in the warmth of his love. "I don't know," she whispered.

"Well, I just wanted to let you know that I love you and want you to go and have fun!" Bashkim said. "But in case you need me, I'm just a phone call away. You can always just slip out of there and I'll come and get you"

It was good to know that she could count on Bashkim for everything. Before him, she didn't have anyone like that in her life. She had never allowed herself to be vulnerable with anyone, yet somehow Bashkim had found his way into her heart.

Since the war, Ariana had been a lone wolf, fiercely independent and unafraid of solitude. Relationships had come and gone like fleeting wisps of smoke, brief encounters that offered temporary break from reality or alleviated her loneliness for a few days. She never revealed her deepest emotions to anyone, never allowing these encounters to blossom into something more meaningful. Yet, she found herself inexplicably drawn into a soulmate-like connection with Bashkim. Their long friendship turned to love after he separated from Suzi, a development that left Ariana feeling conflicted. It was like her common sense had sabotaged her and with age she had felt weakened by loneliness. She suspected that unconsciously, she had craved for closeness and a family like the one Bashkim had with Suzi. Despite her reservations, Bashkim was determined to nurture their relationship beyond friendship, relentlessly pursuing her affection. Still uncertain whether what she felt was truly love, Ariana struggled with conflicting emotions and doubt.

Was it love? she kept asking herself and she didn't know.

"Why me?" She asked Bashkim many times.

"Why choose me to love, when you can have any one of these young women working with us. They would jump at the opportunity."

She couldn't understand why he had fallen in love with her, a woman with a complicated past and a less-than-glamorous present, when he could have had any young and beautiful woman in the world.

"Because I love you, Ariana," he said simply, as if that was all the explanation she needed. She thought back to the countless times he had been there for her, supporting her.

He had witnessed Ariana at her lowest points, during her darkest moments before she even got the job at the office and had never once judged her. He had been the one constant in her life as a friend for a few years now, the only man she could always lean on. Ariana's mind was racing with mixed emotions after Bashkim confessed his feelings for her. Until then, he had been her friend's husband, a figure she respected and admired. Despite this, she couldn't ignore the undeniable connection they shared, their effortless conversations about anything and everything and their mutual dedication to their work at the Ministry of Internal Affairs.

However once he and Suzi separated, she found herself inexplicably drawn to him, offering a listening ear to his woes and taking his side in their separation.

"Why now, Bashkim? Why didn't you say something before? You've known me since you've known Suzi" she asked, her voice trembling with uncertainty.

"I liked you from the moment I saw you with Suzi at that bar, but you never gave me the chance," he replied.

Ariana's heart sank as she thought about Suzi. For months after their separation, she had tried to convince her to give Bashkim another chance at repairing their marriage. Now she found herself caught in the middle of a love triangle.

"Why did you let Suzi believe that you liked her then, that night at the bar?" Ariana demanded to know. "Why be so dishonest?"

"I don't know Ariana" Bashkim admitted "I don't know how any of this happened, but it did, and I am willing to accept things as they are. Are you?"

Ariana felt conflicted. On one hand, she couldn't deny her own growing feelings for Bashkim. On the other hand, she couldn't ignore the potential hurt it would cause her friend if she pursued a relationship with him.

Her head spun as she thought about what to do next. How could she face Suzi? How could she possibly navigate this tangled web of emotions? She was at a point where she couldn't avoid confronting this situation any longer. She came up with two options: she could refuse Bashkim's love and potentially leave her job at the ministry, continue living a lonely life or accept the situation as Bashkim suggested and confess her feelings to Suzi, explaining that they had developed only after her separation from him.

"Tell her the truth," Bashkim had said to her. "She deserves to know. We can't keep hiding like this forever." "I did love her!" Bashkim was adamant in defending himself.

" I didn't plan for any of this to happen. WE ... didn't plan for any of this to happen and you know it!"

"I don't know how to tell her," She sighed .

"Just be honest!" Bashkim kept saying. "She won't care. It won't make a difference to her, if I'm with you or with someone else".

So yes, maybe this was love, Ariana thought. A kind of love that they both needed at this stage in their life. But still, the weight of guilt hung heavily on Ariana's heart, threatening to crush her with its burden. She knew that she couldn't imagine a life without Bashkim and Suzi will forever haunt Ariana's everyday guilt trips. Though she knew that Suzi had moved on, she couldn't shake the feeling that the past that all the three of them shared was an insurmountable obstacle to all their futures.

Ariana had been unaware of their marital turmoil at that time and she had continued to visit them both in their home especially after the birth of their son. She was actually given the role of a godmother to Rron, a lighthearted but important role at the same time, not out of any religious obligation but to honour her unwavering commitment to safeguard the child. The Godmother title was more a funny reference to the movie "The Godfather" than any formal appointment. She didn't know why Suzi had kept her marital problems a secret from her? But she had told her over and over again that life went on no matter what happened between partners and it didn't mean that they had to be tied to one person all their lives.

These cryptic messages that were told to her by Suzi, Ariana always took them as being directed at her as she was refusing to enter into any serious relationship. Little did she know that that was a reflection of Suzi's and Bashkim tumultuous marriage. It was ironic how fate diverged their paths at the same time it seemed. Suzi chose to end her marriage with Bashkim while Ariana got drawn to the wounded husband and father and found herself falling in love with his fractured persona. But the price of stumbling between their fractured relationship was steep. She avoided Suzi at all costs, unable to bear the weight of her friend's judgement and that meant missing their friendship.

"Tonight she will be there for the High School Reunion Party. I won't be able to avoid her. What am I going to say to her?" She thought to herself.

"I don't know if I should go," she said once again to Bashkim on the phone.

"I will let you know. I'll talk to you later"

SEVEN

SUZI

As the first rays of sunlight crept into the room, her phone alarm pierced the peaceful silence, rudely pulling her out of her sleep. It was a familiar routine - setting the alarm on her phone even on the weekends, only to maintain the sanctity of her daily routine. She had grown accustomed to waking up at the same time every day and it was a habit she wasn't willing to break.

The sound of children's voices and laughter drifted in, accompanied by the tantalising aroma of pancakes wafting in from the kitchen. She smiled to herself, knowing that her trusty housekeeper was already at work, keeping things running like clockwork. Despite the mundane nature of her daily routine, she felt an overwhelming sense of gratitude for the little things in life that made it all worth it. She did her best to try and focus only on the little things in life.

As she stood in front of the bathroom mirror, brushing her teeth, the buzz of her old Nokia flip phone, buried deep in her bag, interrupted her. She froze, her heart skipping a beat, knowing that it was not her regular cell phone. "It can't be," she thought, "What would 'they' want from me on a weekend?" With bated breath, she tentatively reached for the phone, her mind racing with thoughts of what the urgent message might be.

She listened to the message in Serbian, her heart pounding in her chest. "Hello! This is urgent! We need to hear from you. We will contact you again tonight, please stand by!" The weight of the message hung heavy in the air as she contemplated its meaning. The serenity of her weekend shattered, replaced with a sense of unease and apprehension. Her mind raced with the implications of what might be asked of her. Her first instinct was to call them back and refuse whatever they wanted, to tell them that she couldn't bear the weight of the secrets any longer. It had been a long time since she had heard from the people that blackmailed her to spy for them. It had been easy at first when she went to the office every day, but lately, she hadn't set foot in the Ministry of the Interior, a job she kept only to say she was employed. She was too afraid of the prying eyes and suspicions of her colleagues. They knew she got that job only because she was the wife of a minister. It was merely a way to keep her occupied and perhaps handle some minor tasks. She never contemplated what would happen if they caught her spying? What if they discovered that she had been copying important emails and gave them to people in Belgrade all these years?

The old Nokia phone in her hand felt like a ticking time bomb, a reminder of the dark secrets she had been keeping. She wanted nothing more than to smash it to pieces, to rid herself of the relentless demands. But she knew she couldn't. She was in it too deep, and the consequences of walking away were too great.

As the weight of the situation bore down on her, a sharp pain pierced her temples, her head throbbing with the stress and anxiety of it all. She closed her eyes, willing the pain to subside, but it only seemed to intensify. It was as though her body was rebelling against the secrets of lies and deceit she had been living with for so long. She knew that she couldn't go on like this forever, that eventually the truth would catch up with her. But for now, she was trapped, unable to break free.

She went to lay down on her bed as she felt weak and dizzy, her mind reeling with the weight of the message. She immediately thought of her son. He was due for a check-up in Belgrade in just two weeks. It was a routine appointment, nothing out of the ordinary, yet thinking of going to Belgrade now felt like a looming threat.

Would they wait for her at the hotel in two weeks, or would they come to find her here at her house if she didn't reply to their message? The thought sent shivers down her spine, knowing that they had eyes and ears everywhere, spies lurking in the shadows, watching her every move. They knew her favourite haunts, her children's schools, her go-to salon, even the name of her doctor. She felt trapped, hemmed in by their knowledge and their reach. She was their prisoner, a pawn in their dangerous game.

As she closed her eyes, the buzzing of the old Nokia phone echoed in her ears and she picked up the phone hurriedly. It was just her imagination this time, as she looked at it intently, trembling. She despised that old phone, the source of so much anxiety and fear. It had been given to her a decade ago in a hotel room in Belgrade, a symbol of her entrapment. She knew that she couldn't escape them, that they would always be one step ahead of her. The weight of it all was suffocating, yet she knew that she had no choice but to carry on. She was a mother, after all, and she would do whatever it took to protect her son.

———

March, 2009

As she lay down on the bed of the old hotel in the centre of Belgrade, with her two-year-old son, Rron, sound asleep beside her, she was startled by a sharp knock. The concierge's voice followed, announcing that there were visitors waiting to see her. She was tired and drained, having just returned from the doctor's office where she had received some troubling news about Rron's health. She didn't have the energy to deal with anyone.

She had noticed something was wrong with Rron a few months earlier. He wouldn't make eye contact with her, and he was always irritable, refusing to smile or engage in any meaningful way. It was like he was trapped in his mind and didn't engage with his surrondings.

The knocks on the door threatened to wake him from his much-needed nap, and she felt a surge of frustration and annoyance. As she made her way to the door, she wondered who could possibly be there to see her. Her grandparents, long deceased, had been the only family she knew in this city. She had hoped to find her mother here, but after some investigation, she had discovered that her mother had left for Canada long ago and was now in an institution, suffering from dementia.

A name flashed through her mind as she reached for the doorknob - Alex. Could it be her brother? She hadn't seen him since that day when he had told her to run for her life up the mountain. Her heart raced and her eyes threatened to betray her as tears welled up at the thought of Alex waiting behind that door. She reached for the knob and as the door flung open, her heart sank like a stone. Instead of Alex, two unknown men in dark grey suits stood before her, one of them clutching a mysterious suitcase.

Confusion engulfed her as she tried to guess who these people were and what did they want? Without waiting for an invitation, they strode past her into the room, their voices crisp and polite. The concierge had already left, and she was alone with these strangers. Panic seized her, and she felt a knot tighten in her stomach. What could she do? Perhaps Bashkim had been right to object to bringing their son to the military academy hospital in Belgrade, but desperation had driven her to beg him to let her come. There was no one else who could help her son in Kosovo, she was sure of that. She had obtained a Serbian passport for herself, eager to do whatever it took to get her son the medical care he needed. After all, she was half-Serbian, and no one could deny her to get the passport of the country where her mother was born.

As she watched the two men make themselves at home, she couldn't shake the feeling that her world was about to turn upside down. "I shouldn't be afraid," she repeated to herself, steeling her nerves and turning around to confront the two imposing figures who had brazenly entered her room uninvited. With a sharp edge to her voice, she demanded to know who they were and how they had the audacity to barge into her personal space.

Keeping a watchful eye on her son, she held the door open and waited for their response, her heart pounding in her chest like a drumbeat.

"Don't be afraid," the older man spoke up, his voice calm and measured. "We just want to talk to you. It's better here than taking you down to the police station. We don't want to inconvenience you." His words made her shiver, but the younger man's gentler tone helped to soothe her jangled nerves. "We know who you are," he said, his voice soft and reassuring. "We just want to ask you some questions. Please," he added, extending his hand and offering her one of the chairs in the room. With trepidation and uncertainty, she slowly closed the door and took a seat, feeling like a helpless pawn in a game she didn't understand. For over an hour, they talked, probing her with questions and listening intently to her responses. She tried to remain composed, but fear and uncertainty gnawed at her insides, leaving her feeling raw and vulnerable. She listened in silence, her gaze fixed on her sleeping son, the weight of the two men's words heavy on her shoulders. They knew everything, too much about her family, her heritage, and her work. They had a proposition for her, one that she couldn't refuse.

"Your father was a good Albanian" they told her "And your brother, a good Serb, a hero". "It's your turn to help us get revenge on those that destroyed everything that you loved."

She looked at her son again, her hands shaking and tears coming to her eyes.

They made sure she understood that she didn't have a choice.

Her throat dried up but she didn't really know what to say. Tears welled up in her eyes as she tried to comprehend the magnitude of what they were asking of her.

They just wanted her to forward them some emails from her husband's computer, they said. Since she was also a worker at the ministry, she shouldn't have any problem accessing information that they wanted. She would be rewarded with protection and a free hotel room every time she came to Belgrade and the medical bills of her son would be paid in full.

With a quivering voice, she tried to refuse, but they were insistent. They made it clear that her compliance was non-negotiable. Fear and desperation filled her as she thought about her son's safety.

"Thank you, Thank you very much but I don't really need help with anything" she started to say but they interrupted her "We insist!" The older guy said.

"You have a wonderful son" the younger guy said walking towards the bed where Rron was sleeping.

She stood up "Please!" She said in a weak voice "Please don't hurt my son." "I'll do anything you want me to."

"Oh no! Of course I won't hurt him" he said with a sneer. "I'm just admiring him and noticing how much he looks like your brother Alex."

"Where is Alex?" she gathered the courage to ask. "Is he alive?"

"To be honest, I don't know" the young guy said "He just disappeared after the war." "I fought with him in Kosovo, that's how I knew him but never saw him since."

Suzi looked at him intently and she didn't believe him. Just a few minutes ago he was talking as if he saw her brother just yesterday.

"Will you help me find him if I agree to help you?" she dared to ask.

"Sure" the guy said nonchalantly, grinning at her sarcastically. "I'll see what I can do."

She was in no position to bargain or insist on anything, so she didn't say anything anymore. Looking at her son sleeping peacefully in the bed, she knew she had to do everything they asked of her.

They gave her a phone and arranged to meet with her every few months, at the time of the doctor's appointments. In between appointments, they called her with instructions if needed and she often left printed copies of documents and other information at an address in Gracanice, near the Serbian Orthodox Monastery on the outskirts of Prishtina.

From that day on, she lived in constant fear, never knowing when the next message or meeting would come.

———

The weight of the phone message lingered heavily on her mind, a reminder of the dangerous game she was playing. She tried to calm herself, telling herself that she had done this countless times before. But the fear and anxiety still gnawed at her insides. She knew what she had to do. Wait for the right opportunity to open Bashkim's emails, take pictures of them with her small phone, and forward them to those men. If they needed documents, she would have to quickly photocopy the necessary files and discreetly drop them herself to a house not too far from her home.

Come Monday, she would go to the office and tell Bashkim that she wanted to show her face there, from time to time, out of guilt for not showing up for work and she would get whatever information they wanted this time, she told herself trying to calm down. But her thoughts kept drifting back to all the insistent demands they were making lately. What could they want now? The thought nagged at her endlessly.

She had a good idea of their interests: the American Embassies correspondence with the Kosovo government, and the schedule of meetings and their locations. But there was always the fear that they would want something more, something that she might not be able to deliver, therefore putting her family in danger. The thought was paralysing. In an attempt to take these worries off her mind and stay focused on the evening ahead, she got dressed quickly and drove herself to the hairdresser appointment. They loved her there. They always treated her like a princess and she always left them a big tip.

Suzi stepped into the salon, breathing in the rich and luxurious atmosphere. The air was heavy with the scent of expensive perfumes and the sound of soft music filled her ears. She was greeted by the most prestigious hairdresser in town, a man who had built a reputation as the best in the business. As she took her seat in one of the tastefully decorated booths, he approached her with a gentle smile and ordered a young girl to bring Suzi a cappuccino, her usual drink.

"Hey sweetie" the overly dramatic hairdresser greeted her with a big smile and he carefully made a kissing sound "muah, muah"... close to both her cheeks.

"So good to see you," he said. Suzi sank back into the plush seat, feeling relaxed and pampered. The salon was exclusive, with a strong emphasis on privacy, and every customer was made to feel like the most important person in the room. The staff moved quietly around the room, tending to the needs of their clients with skill and precision. The atmosphere was calm and serene, and for a moment, Suzi felt as though she had escaped the pressures of the world outside.

"I heard you're going to the reunion party tonight. That must be so exciting" the hairdresser said. "Yes, I'm looking forward to it," she replied as the hairdresser began working his magic on her locks. She closed her eyes, enjoying the sensation of the warm water and skilled fingers massaging her scalp.

It had been a while since she saw some of her old classmates from high school and she was feeling a little nervous about it, she told him.

The hairdresser continued chatting with her, asking about her life and how things were going and Suzi felt a sense of comfort and familiarity with him. Maybe it was the fact that he knew just how to make her hair look its best, or maybe it was his genuine interest in her life that made her feel at ease. As she sipped her cappuccino and let herself relax, Suzi realised that this was the only place where she could truly be herself. Here she could safely take off the mask, and be as vulnerable as she wanted, talking endlessly about her everyday life, though not her secrets. In the booths of this salon, she felt like her most genuine self.

High school reunion parties had become the talk of the town and were viewed as pivotal events in the social calendar. The allure of these soirées was so irresistible that even those who had fled the country as refugees would return from far-flung corners of the world to attend. No one wanted to miss out on these extravagant events, and with each passing year, the festivities grew more lavish. From the venues to the live entertainment, decorations, and sumptuous cuisine, everything was executed with the utmost care to ensure an unforgettable experience. Each successive year, the pressure to outdo the previous celebration became more intense as every generation competed to leave a lasting impression.

The photos from these festivities flooded social media every year, each image capturing the joy of old friends reunited after so many years of turmoil. The survivors of the war felt an overwhelming need to celebrate the life they had almost lost and to see each other again. They also used these events to honour and remember the friends they lost in the war.

For some, the years between their final class at high school and this reunion had been marked by successes and triumphs, while others had struggled with the lasting trauma of the past. The reunion also provided a chance for some people that still fought with depression and loneliness to reconnect with old friends, while Suzi, generally speaking, was simply just curious to find out about what became of everyone. Judging from the photos she had seen on Facebook, it seemed to her that everyone at the reunion was united by a sense of nostalgia for the life they had before the war, before everything turned upside down and ugly. Though they were far from old, the years of their childhood and youth felt like a whole lifetime away, a distant memory that they could only recall in flashes. This was certainly the case for Suzi.

The hair salon's calming ambiance and pampering staff had always been a refuge for Suzi, but today, her thoughts kept drifting elsewhere. Her usually chatty hairdresser noticed her silence and attempted to coax her into conversation, to no avail. Sensing something amiss, he probed gently, "Is something wrong?" Suzi hesitated for a moment before revealing, "It's just that I've been a bit stressed out in the past few days." With a sympathetic smile, the hairdresser suggested a massage from the next-door masseuse, who he promised had "hands of gold." But Suzi's mind was too preoccupied for indulgences, and she declined half-heartedly, lost in her thoughts. Undeterred, the hairdresser continued to boost her spirits. "Relax and remember, sweetie, you will be the best looking tonight. Your high school friends won't believe their eyes when they see how wonderful you look. Just smile!" His words had a way of lifting her mood, and as she gazed at her reflection, she had to admit that she did look stunning but despite her outward appearance, she felt drained, the weight of her worries clinging on her like a millstone around her neck. She felt like she was still running up that mountain where her brother had left her and saved her life. She felt the weight of the mountain on her, its steep incline and jagged terrain as daunting as the memories it held. She also still felt the flames of destruction licking at her heels, a reminder of the inferno that had ravaged her father's village and consumed everything in it.

The flames that had taken her grandparents, her country and all her loved ones, leaving her alone and unprotected in a world that was far too cruel. On her way back from the salon, she furtively retrieved the concealed phone and played the message once more. The urgency in the voice on the other end was frightening, making her anxious again. She knew without a doubt that the stakes were high, and that her situation was dire. As she replayed the message over and over again, a disturbing realisation slowly dawned on her. "They" had never left a message before. They had always persisted in calling until she answered. This was different, and she couldn't shake the unease that crept into her heart. She felt that something was off, that the game had changed in ways she wasn't yet aware of. The sunken feeling in her gut only deepened, filling her with trepidation about what could be lying ahead.

EIGHT

FATIME

As the moon still lingered in the sky, casting a soft glow through the window, she stirred from her sleep. She had a feeling like she had only slept for a few minutes. It was a familiar feeling, one that she had grown accustomed to over time. The clock read 4:00 am every day when she opened her eyes. She never needed an alarm to wake up. With practised efficiency, she slipped out of bed and got her clothes, tiptoeing down the hallway towards the bathroom. The cool tiles felt refreshing under her feet as she took a quick shower, washing away the last remnants of sleep from her body. She dressed in silence, not wanting to disturb Agim or his mother.

In the kitchen, she went about her morning routine: putting the kettle on and boiling some eggs for breakfast. She put some bread and cheese on the table, arranging them neatly as she always did. The ritual of working quietly alone was usually comforting but not today. Today, a mixture of excitement and fear coursed through her body, creating a tingling sensation that seemed to electrify every nerve. She wondered what the day held in store for her, but knew deep down that her wishes and decisions were not entirely within her control. They were usually determined by Agim's and his mother's whims. What if, in a sudden change of heart, Agim forbade her from visiting her mother today? What if he deemed it unnecessary or inconvenient, thus crushing her eager anticipation to realise her plans: attend the high school reunion and get on the bus to Sarande first thing tomorrow morning and never come back to this house again. The mere possibility of not being able to go through with her plan made her shiver, and she prayed slowly that such a fate would not befall her.

She longed for the freedom to chart her own course, to make her own decisions without fear of retribution or denial. But for now, she was at the mercy of others, her fate in their hands. As the clock ticked closer to 4:40, she heard Agim waking up and heading to the bathroom. He was preparing for the morning prayers, as he always did.

She always prayed in the same room with him, always hoping that the ritual will bring them together one day. But he always ignored her. The guest room where they prayed was vast and empty, and she could not help but feel small and insignificant in the face of its size and in the fact that Agim always pretended not to see her praying in the corner behind him. Agim moved up and down, his movements slow and deliberate as he quietly mouthed the prayers in Arabic. They had both learned them by heart, reciting them with reverence and devotion. Today, Fatime was just mechanically moving up and down, absentmindedly. When Agim finished his prayers, he always remained seated for a few minutes more, his eyes closed as he waited for her to exit the room first. So that's what she did today, too.

After breakfast, Fatime prepared for her journey. She put on her hijab and took her carefully packed duffle bag with her and waited for Agim to tell her when the taxi would arrive. He would accompany her in the taxi, all the way to the front door of the building where her mother lived, and then return home in the same taxi.

Ever since his religious infatuation had taken hold, he had become increasingly strict with her, forbidding her from going anywhere alone. As she stood there, waiting for Agim to give the signal, a twinge of sadness washed over her. Her gaze swept over every corner of her bedroom, her sanctuary, then downstairs to the kitchen and the hallway. Each step reverberated with a lifetime of memories and emotions, a testament to the years of sacrifice and perseverance she had invested in this home. So many wasted years, she thought. All for nothing. As she reached the front door, a strange sense of liberation stirred within her, as though she were shedding an old skin to embrace a new, unfamiliar reality. For too long, she had been weighed down by the chains of expectation, by the burden of fulfilling obligations that she never truly believed in. She had this strange feeling of rebirth, of leaving her old self behind continuing to toil endlessly inside that house while the new Fatime that she had waited so long to bring back to life was already emerging in her mind. A flame of determination flickered in her soul.

As she sat alone in the backseat of the taxi, while Agim sat in front next to the driver, she imagined how nice it would be if Agim would sit next to her in the back seat and maybe hold her hand, like he used to. Oh, how she wished he would tell her that he too had suffered in silence, that he too yearned for a return to the carefree love they had once shared. Her mind plagued by a thousand unanswered questions, she longed for a glimpse into the darkness that had consumed Agim for all these years. She wished with all her heart that he would confide his pain and his secrets to her, that he would share the horrors of his time in prison, the pain and suffering that had eroded his spirit. She yearned to know what the police had done to him, what unspeakable atrocities had been inflicted on his body and soul. And yet, she knew that he would never reveal anything, not even a single word. . She knew that the scars of his past were too deep and that she'd been unable to unlock that door all these years.

And so, she sat quietly, looking down at her feet, her heart heavy with the weight of pain and the anguish that had filled their lives. She closed her eyes and imagined a vision of the man she had once loved so deeply, the man who had filled her life with laughter and joy. A part of her felt like a failure who had finally given up trying to bring Agim back.

As she stepped out of the taxi, her heart heavy with unspoken pain, her eyes brimmed with tears that threatened to spill over. Without looking at him, she murmured a soft farewell, her eyes downcast. She couldn't bear to look at the man who had once been her everything and then for so many years was a stranger to her.

As she walked towards her mother's apartment building, her mind was awash with conflicting emotions. She longed to finally leave behind the life of pain and sorrow that had consumed her for so long. And yet, she couldn't help but feel a deep sense of regret, a sense of great loss.

She entered the apartment block and climbed the stairs, a wave of relief washed over her. She ripped off her hijab, letting her long black hair fall down her back, and wiped away her tears. Excitement coursed through her veins as she rang the bell, eager to see the one person who could soothe her troubled heart. As her mother opened the door, her warm smile lighting up the room, she rushed forward to embrace her, the weight of her troubles falling away. For a few moments, she stood there, in her mother's warm embrace, her body slowly relaxing. It will take her a while to adjust to the normalcy of life outside the confines of strict religious observation but she was ready to try. She took a deep breath and followed her mother into the small apartment that had once been her home. She was going to rest and then get ready for the party later that evening.

———

Fatime sat across from her mother, sipping her coffee, and wondered how she was going to tell her mother about what she was about to do. How much should she reveal? The secret was burning inside her. She knew her mother would worry, would fret and fuss over her plans, and she wasn't sure if she was ready to deal with that.

Taking a deep breath, she cleared her throat and began, "Do you remember my school friend Besa?" Her mother's face lit up with recognition, a smile spreading across her lips.

"Of course, my dear. Such a nice girl! I wonder what happened to her? Didn't she go to America and marry an American?"

"Yes, she did," said Fatime.

"Whenever I see America in the news, I think of her," Her mother said.

" Well, she's come home to Prishtine and she has invited me and a few other friends to go out with her tonight," said Fatime.

"Oh how nice! exclaimed her mother and clapped her hands with joy not really paying close attention to parts of the sentence.

"I'm so happy for her mother. Poor woman! All alone. How much she suffered in life. Her only daughter, living in America. I'm so happy Besa came to see her." she was going on and on..

Fatime shifted in her seat, taking a sip of her coffee as her mother continued to gush over Besa's return. Then she stopped for a moment, a frown crossing her brow as she seemed puzzled. "How did she get in touch with you?" she asked.

"You bought me a phone, remember?"

"I thought, you never use it except to call me. Agim doesn't know you have a phone. No one does. How did Besa find your number?" Her mother asked again, puzzled.

" I have a social media account," Fatime admitted to her mother reluctantly.

Her mother was still confused.

"A Facebook account? I never saw you there."

"Oh mom, I have a Fake social media account and you are not my friend there."

This will be hard to explain, Fatime thought; she hated it when her mom found out she was keeping secrets from her. She got really offended when that happened. So Fatime started explaining to her mother how she stumbled upon the announcement of her high school reunion party on social media, thanks to the phone that she had bought for her a year ago. She really wanted to attend it, she told her mother and she kept it a secret from everyone because she knew that attending such an event would be frowned upon in her conservative community. The thought of seeing her old classmates again after all these years was too tempting, she told her mother.

With a sense of clandestine excitement, she had kept the phone hidden from everyone, knowing that if she was caught, she would be met with disapproval and questions she couldn't answer. Agim, her husband, had been strict about their religious and cultural customs, including his disdain for the internet. As a "proper Muslim" woman, according to him, Fatime shouldn't be wasting her time online.

But online, in the labyrinths of the virtual world, Fatime discovered a world that she had long yearned for. The marvels of technology unfolded before her like a divine intervention, a gift sent from God straight into her hands. Trapped in the confines of her home, her hunger for knowledge and connections with the outside world was enormeous. She finally found freedom beyond her imagination, a whole new universe that opened up to her with all the knowledge in the world. The vast and endless expanse of possibilities that opened up before her was just like the universe itself opening up before her. She could finally reach all the knowledge and freedom that she craved for thanks to the smartphone her mother had given her. She felt like she went back to the classroom again where she had been a star. It was the most precious gift that she had ever received and it transformed her life. For Fatime, the internet was not just a source of entertainment or social interaction. It was her refuge, a means to escape from the mundane and oppressive reality of her daily life. The endless possibilities and connections with the outside world at her fingertips and the freedom to be whoever she wanted and to express herself online had given her a sense of empowerment that she had only felt at school but a millions fold that.

It was through the internet that she had discovered the high school reunion event, which in turn had led to her decision to take control of her life exactly on this day.

She had opened her Facebook Account a few days after her mother gave her the phone. One afternoon, after her mother in law took her usual nap, she went to her room and started using the internet on the phone her mother paid for every month. While scrolling through an online newspaper, she stumbled upon an article that caught her eye. It was a guide on how to open a social media account, complete with step-by-step instructions and helpful tips. At first, she was hesitant. The idea of putting herself out there for the world to see was out of the question, and the thought of navigating the complex world of social media without revealing herself was daunting. But as she read on, a sense of curiosity began to stir within her. What if she could connect with people, without ever leaving home? What if she could share her thoughts, ideas, and experiences with others, and learn from theirs in return? With trembling fingers, she clicked on the link and began the process of creating her account. She knew she had to create a fake account so no one could identify her, so the name she chose for herself on Facebook had to be perfect. It needed to be modern, appealing, and, most importantly, reflect who she truly was. Her grandmother's name, Fatime, given to her by her father, had always felt like a burden. It seemed to belong to a different time and world, and from a young age, she had wished for a different name. She never knew her grandmother, but the name had always felt foreign to her, as if it belonged only to the woman in the faded photos of her father's family album. When her mother called her by that name, it always took her a few seconds to respond because she didn't think of herself as Fatime. The name conjured images of a nice elderly woman, not the person she felt she was. And so, she settled on the name Saranda, a name that had been swirling around in her mind for as long as she could remember. It was the name of a place she had never been to but had always longed to visit; a name she would have liked to name her daughter if she had one. Saranda, a coastal city in Albania, was a place of wonder and beauty, a place that had captured her heart through the countless photos and videos of the place she had seen on TV. The houses perched on top of hills, overlooking the sparkling turquoise water of the Ionian Sea, had seemed like something out of a dream. And the name, oh the name! It rolled off her tongue like a melody, a magical word that held within it the promise of a brighter world. She knew many girls in Kosovo named Saranda, but in the moment that she wrote down that name for her Facebook account , she felt like the only one, a shining star in a universe that was all her own. In choosing this name for herself on social media, she had taken the first step towards claiming a new identity for herself, towards forging a path that was uniquely hers. And as she hit the "submit" button, a sense of joy and liberation had flooded her soul. Oh the magic of being on social media was indescribable.

As Fatime had sat with her smart phone day after day for a couple of hours a day, her heart had fluttered with a sense of newfound freedom. Gone were the days of feeling stifled, trapped in a world that didn't understand or value her. Now, she could explore any topic that piqued her interest, delve deep into discussions and debates, and seek out answers to questions that had long troubled her. With a touch of a button, she could access newspapers and magazines from all corners of the globe, immersing herself in different cultures and ways of thinking. And the greatest gift of all was the ability to learn. With free online courses at her fingertips, Fatime's thirst for knowledge was quenched like never before. It was as though the universe had conspired to bring her this opportunity, and she felt a deep sense of gratitude towards God for blessing her with such abundance.

Every day, she eagerly awaited the precious hours when her mother-in-law would take her nap, allowing Fatime to steal away to her room and get online. Since then her steps became lighter and her mood lifted, blissful by the promise of discovery and growth.

She didn't know how she was going to explain all this to her mother, so she decided she wouldn't even try.

The air was thick with tension as Fatime's mother looked at her with a stern gaze.

"I'm happy you're using the phone to get in touch with your friends," her mother said. "Did you tell Agim that you are going out with your friends?" she asked, her voice tinged with disapproval.

Fatime remained calm and composed, refusing to let her mother's disapproving tone get to her. There was so much she didn't know about her marriage so Fatime wasn't going to get mad or offended by her mother's attitude.

"No, I didn't," she replied evenly. "And it's not just going out, it's the High School Reunion Party." a small smile crept onto her lips.

Her mother's eyes widened in shock. "Oh my God," she exclaimed. "Why didn't you tell me?"

Fatime couldn't help but roll her eyes inwardly. High School Reunion Parties were a big deal, a social event that required weeks of planning and preparation. It was no wonder that her mother was offended that Fatime hadn't discussed it with her beforehand. Her mother started to panic as Fatime thought about how to calm her down.

"What if Agim finds out about the party? You were in the same class. His friends will see you and tell him that you were there?" Her mother's voice was laced with hysteria now, her concern spiralling out of control.

But Fatime refused to let her mother's anxiety infect her own resolve. "He won't find out," she said firmly, her tone leaving no room for argument.

"He doesn't go out at night. He doesn't have any friends that knew him before the war, and he wouldn't recognize me even if he saw me with his own eyes."

Her mother was incredulous. "What do you mean? Of course he would."

But Fatime was confident in her plan. "I will wear the dress that you bought for me for Prom night that never happened," she said, a faint smile crossing her lips. "I know you kept it all these years. It will still fit me. I will do my hair and put on some makeup. No hijab. He will not recognize me even if I came face to face with him."

For a moment, her mother was speechless, her gasp echoing in the silence. But she said nothing, her expression a mix of concern and understanding. And with that, Fatime knew that she had won the argument. If her mother only knew how much she was looking forward to attending the High School Reunion party, she wouldn't be so hard on her for sure. It had been too long since she had seen her dearest friends, the ones she had not laid eyes on since the early days of Spring in '99 when they were told Schools were closed and they should stay home and stay safe. She would have never imagined her life would turn out the way it did.

Going to the reunion party she hoped to get a glimpse of her past life, a glimpse of who she once was in High School, before the devastation of war befell, before she exchanged vows and took on a role she never could have fathomed.

The reunion party was more than just a gathering of old classmates; it was a window into her past soul, she thought, a chance to reminisce and reclaim the person she once was. The thought of walking through the doors of a banquet hall and seeing the familiar faces with whom she had shared memories of childhood, made her heart skip a beat. She felt a mixture of emotions wash over her-nostalgia, hope, and apprehension all intermingled in her heart. The memories of her youth flooded her mind, filling her with a sense of longing that she couldn't quite shake. She wanted to step back in time, even if just for one night, to relive the moments that had shaped her young life. Tonight was a chance to reconnect with her younger self and perhaps even rediscover parts of herself that she had lost along the way.

———

Fatime's mother, a retired nurse with an updo shellacked with hairspray, had always been a pillar of strength and wisdom in her life. Despite Fatime's conservative in law's wishes, she had urged her daughter not to surrender her independence or her identity. "Remember, my love," she had said, "you don't need to veil yourself to be a true Muslim, and you don't need religion to be a good person. Our generation believed in socialism, in gender equality and I can't believe the children now seem to go back in the time of my grandmother". During years, her mother grew increasingly concerned for her well-being. She saw the misery on her face, the weight of a failing marriage crushing her spirit. She begged her to leave Agim, to come live with her and her brother's family. "You're not an orphan, my dear," she implored. "You don't have to bear this suffering alone." Despite her mother's advice, Fatime had clung to the hope that Agim would return to his former self, to the man she had fallen in love with. Moreover, she could not bear to burden her family with the weight of her financial and emotional struggles. War had changed everything, turning their world upside down and tearing apart the very fabric of their lives. No one was spared the pain and the suffering, and Fatime was no exception. The trials of war had left her scarred, both physically and emotionally, and had deepened the chasm between her and Agim. But she knew she couldn't just burden her family, who were struggling to make ends meet, by adding another mouth to feed. Her mother and brother's family lived in a small, cramped apartment, with very limited space. It was a small, modest one, barely big enough to accommodate her brother's growing family. The living room, which served as both a common area and a bedroom, was dominated by two couches, where she and her mother would sleep whenever she came for a few days' visit. She knew that her presence was an imposition, a burden on an already overcrowded living conditions. Her brother, his wife, and their two young children occupied the only bedroom in the apartment. She knew how hard it was for them to make ends meet and cope with the daily struggles.

The memory of the high school prom, which had never taken place because of the war, lingered in Fatime's mind like a wistful dream. She had mourned the loss of that special occasion for years. She remembered fondly the dress that her mother had purchased for her despite their financial hardship and that was still hanging unused in her mother's closet.

"I want to wear the Prom Dress that I never got to wear" she told her mother.

"I think it will fit me perfectly. What do you think?" she asked again.

She imagined the dress fitting like a glove, the soft fabric embracing her lean body and flowing gracefully around her feet. She would style her hair, artfully arranging it in a way that framed her face and accentuated her natural beauty. She would apply just the right amount of makeup, enhancing her features and adding a touch of allure to her appearance. She had planned everything.

"Ok" said her mother, still in a bit of shock.

"I'll go and find the dress" then she stood up and opened the door of one of the closets that were lined up in a row in the living room. The clothes were carefully and neatly folded in the drawers. She seemed to know exactly where Fatime's Prom dress was. It took her only a minute to find it. As Fatime gazed into her mother's eyes, she could sense a tumultuous mix of emotions churning within her. Excitement, tinged with fear and anticipation, radiated from her every pore, a testament to the deep concern she felt for her. And yet, despite this natural concern, her mother refrained from asking the question that loomed large in both their minds: had Fatime left Agim for good?

Perhaps it was the fear of the unknown that held her mother back, the worry of how her son and daughter-in-law would react to the news of Fatime living here with them. On the other hand, Fatime knew that her mother was happy if she was happy. She had wanted her happiness for so many years now.

Her mother would be consumed with worry if she knew the truth, that Fatime would be leaving for Sarande immediately after the party. And so, with a heavy heart, she resolved to keep this information to herself, to spare her mother the agony of further concern.

Her mother moved quickly to get Fatime's dress freshened up and iron it.

She hadn't seen her daughter wearing a party dress for a very long time.

NINE

THE EVE OF THE REUNION

THE REUNION - June, 2019

With a graceful skip, Besa jumped on a taxi, her heart alight with joy. Settling in the back seat, she flashed a radiant smile at the handsome young driver. To her delight, he returned the gesture, and she felt a warm flush spread across her cheeks.

As he inquired about her destination, his use of the formal address "ma'am" towards her, momentarily caught her off guard. Glancing up at his reflection showing in the mirror of the car, she took a moment to scrutinise her own appearance in a small hand held mirror that she took out from her bag and quickly glanced at herself unnoticed by the driver. Had she truly reached the point in life where addressing her as ma'am was appropriate? She smiled at this thought. Composing herself and taking a deep breath, she replied, "At Sheshi 21, please," all the while maintaining a charming smile. He met her gaze in the mirror, with a smile that she found adorable. A moment of silence lingered between them. "Does the soul ever get old?" Besa thought to herself. She was ageing for sure but she wasn't addressed as ma'am until now and this was surprising as well as amusing.

Interrupting her thoughts, the driver spoke up once more, asking if she was going to the Reunion Party. It seemed everyone in town knew about the event. Besa confirmed that the party was indeed her destination. "Did you come from abroad to attend it?" he asked next, looking at her through the mirror. She hesitated a bit and then she said "Yes, I've come from the US three days ago"

With a discerning eye, he commented on her unique sense of style, a welcomed deviation from the norm, he said. He could tell by her modest style that she lived abroad. "The ladies here watch too much TV" he commented smiling "and probably get their styling ideas from the soap operas' '. They both laughed. She forgot for a moment his persistent use of "ma'am,". As the conversation continued, she felt a strange mix of gratitude and confusion, uncertain of how to respond to the driver's charm and courtesy. She didn't know yet that the charming and chatting cab drivers were another new distinctiveness of the city. She quite enjoyed this frendliness and contrary to her initial apprehension, Besa felt a flutter of excitement within her, akin to that of a high schooler attending prom for the very first time. Determined to savour every moment, she tried to make small conversation while taking in the sights of the city and commenting on them with the driver.

As she peered out the car window, the city lights began to flicker past her, casting a kaleidoscope of colours against the sky. The sunset hues of pink and blue painted a mesmerising backdrop, lending an ethereal quality to the scene.

Her gaze drifted towards the familiar streets that they passed, and she couldn't help but feel a sense of nostalgia wash over her once again. It was as though she had drifted back to her youth, almost seeing herself out there walking down those very same streets, in a completely different time. Besa's mind drifted to the many events and memories of her youth that were woven into the fabric of the city. The taxi drove her past familiar landmarks which held a special place in her heart. She recalled the Sports Center, where she and her friends had staged a hunger strike in solidarity with Trepca Mine workers. It was a time of great turmoil and upheaval in her country, and Besa had been consumed with righteous anger at the injustice that surrounded her. Passing by the University Building, her thoughts turned to the day when Albanian students and teachers were barred from attending classes. She remembered the heart-breaking scenes of students being forcibly removed from the premises by police. As the taxi made its way towards the city centre, memories of carefree evenings spent with friends came flooding back. The bustling main square, or Korzo as they affectionately called it, was a hub of activity and entertainment. They would stroll from one end of the square to the other, indulging in ice cream, popcorn, and black seeds, hoping to catch a glimpse of seniors of their high school who never noticed them. Besa smiled wistfully at the memories. Despite the challenges and struggles that surrounded them, Besa and her friends had always held onto the simple pleasures of youth. They had refused to be defeated by the harsh realities of their world, choosing to believe in a brighter future and a better tomorrow. They had never imagined that their carefree days would be shattered by the horrors of war. It was a surreal and bewildering time, as the world that they had known and thought would get better with work and understanding, was replaced by one that was totally unrecognisable,frightening and cruel. She now realised that without the sacrifice of war, this new freedom and democracy would have never come. She was mournful of her lost youth but glad that the people here finally got rid of the oppressive system and were free. You could see it in the way they walked down the streets, in groups laughing and smiling. The city was like a college campus and these new "kids" were free and had no major calamities coming over them. She felt grateful for that.

Besa gazed at the young taxi driver; his black hair neatly trimmed and his white collar crisp and clean. She realised that, in some ways, she truly was a ma'am - so much time had passed since the events of her youth that they now seemed like ancient history. She scrutinised the driver's youthful features, noting how different his experience of the world must be from her own. Most likely, he was born after the war, too young to remember the devastation and destruction that had plagued their country. She envied him for that, for in some ways, she wished she could see the world with his eyes - eyes that had not been scarred by the horrors of war.

A nice song was playing on the radio and she could feel the young man's glances at her from the car mirror.

"Hey girl friend,
    The day you said you were leaving
    My voice and my soul went silent
    I know you will never come back here again ..."
    The song said.

As the lyrics of the song filled the car, Besa couldn't wait to see all the new developments in the city, to get to work, and to meet all the energetic and vibrant young people. Starting her new journey with the reunion event seemed like a perfect way to begin this new chapter of her life.

———

After trying on all three or four fancy dresses in her closet, Ariana finally decided on the red one. It made her feel strong somehow. She never wanted people to feel sorry for her or see her only as a war victim. She had long ago decided that war and tragedies would not define her. She held her grief and sorrow tightly to her chest. No one knew her story and no one saw her pain. One had to look very closely, deep into her big black eyes, to notice the perpetual sadness hidden inside. Her eyes were like a deep, bottomless well, carefully made up to seem seductive instead of sad. Her thick eyelashes always fanned her tears, never letting them fall on her face. Her lips were always painted in deep red lipstick. This, in a way, was her mask, one that she put on every day, to seem "normal" or happy, or unbothered, unfazed, even dumb or easygoing, or flirty and seductive... depending on the situation. People talked behind her back, and she knew it but she never wanted to give anyone the satisfaction of feeling sorry for her because she had already lost everything in life and she wasn't going to let other people's opinions make her lose her sense of self too.

The more people talked, the feistier she became - the redder her lipstick, the darker her eyes, the higher her heels. Some even dared to blame her for Arben's death.

"If she hadn't convinced him to run away that day, he wouldn't be gone. She sent him straight to his death,"they said. "She made that boy crazy with her devilish eyes," they said.

"And look at her now, she doesn't care. Not about him and not about her whole family, that went after her, never to be found again, either dead or alive. "How could she?" they said. "Marre" (Shame) they said. "Kurvë" (Whore) they said.

She knew all those people would have been so much happier if she had wailed and died in her grief somewhere on the side of a street. She knew people wanted to pity her, to feel sorry for her, perhaps to throw some coins at her feet and then feel good about themselves. But no, she refused to give them that satisfaction. She was a survivor and surviving was what she had to do. "Djali jem" (My son) the words of her father echoed in her ears all the time.

The red dress brought her best features. Who could look into her eyes when she wore that dress? "No one," she thought. She still had doubts whether she would be able to enter the party room and face all those people. She might change her mind and return home once she saw the crowds but for now she was going to get ready. She would See how she felt when she got near the venue.

Despite her doubts that had gripped her earlier, Ariana arrived at the venue half an hour early. She sat in her car, her heart pounding with apprehension, her palms sweating as she tried to gather courage to venture inside. It took her a while to muster the willpower to get out of the car, but eventually, she did.

Once outside, she decided to wait for Besa in front of the building, pacing nervously and chain-smoking cigarettes as she scanned the crowd. She was tempted to look at the sea of unfamiliar faces that had already flooded the entrance;instead,she focused on her phone intently.

Besa had asked her to wait for her at the door, and Ariana had readily agreed, relieved at the prospect of not having to navigate the intimidating scene at the lobby all by herself. As she stood there, with each minute ticking away, she felt a tremendous sense of unease.

From the earliest days of their childhood, Besa had been a towering presence in her life. Her influence on her was big, even now after not seeing each other for so many years, she still was worried that she might unwittingly let her down, leading to the dissolution of their friendship. As a little girl, she had followed Besa around like a shadow, emulating her every move, and longing to dress and speak like her. Besa, in Ariana's eyes, was always the wiser, more mature of the two. Now, as Ariana stood outside the venue, her mind was consumed with doubts and insecurities. What if Besa didn't recognize her? Or worse yet, what if she was disappointed with the way she looked when she saw her in real life after all these years? Her anxieties were compounded by the uncertainty of whether she still looked like the woman in the photographs she had sent Besa not long ago. The mere thought of seeing her old friend again, after all these years, filled her with a mix of excitement and trepidation.

As the moments stretched on, Ariana's nerves were getting to the point of overwhelming her completely. She clutched her package of cigarettes, and lit another one. Her thoughts were spinning in a whirlwind, a mixture of emotions and anxieties that refused to go away. All of a sudden she felt an urge to cry and as she fought to keep her tears at bay, wiping her nose repeatedly, opening and closing her bag in a bid to distract herself. Her impatience grew, intensifying with every passing moment. She thought of leaving and was heading to her car but then, at long last, she saw the taxi approaching. Her heart leapt as she recognized Besa in an instant. The woman in the taxi was the adult embodiment of the face she knew so well, her dear friend from childhood. Ariana's relief was instant, her fears ebbed away. Besa was finally here, and nothing else mattered.

———

Suzi struggled to shake off the weight of her anxiety, her mind shrouded in a thick fog. The burden of her secret intensified by the thought of the message on her phone this morning, seemed to grow heavier with each passing moment. She longed to confide in someone, anyone. But alas, she knew she was unable to share her worries and fears with anyone. As she stood in front of the bathroom mirror for the fourth time that day, she played back the phone message once more, her heart heavy with despair. "I can't take this anymore," she whispered to herself, the words ringing hollow. In a moment of desperation, she considered calling Bashkim, to tell him everything and ask for his help. The thought of unburdening herself to him was a tantalising prospect. She found herself staring at his number on her phone, the digits staring back at her intently. She hesitated, her finger hovering over the button, before ultimately deciding against it. Suzi's mind was fraught with questions, each one more ominous than the last. Would Bashkim understand her plight and offer comfort and a solution, or would he lash out at her, branding her a traitor and an enemy of the state? Would he accuse her of endangering the lives of their family and her fellow citizens? The mere thought of it made her heart race with anxiety. She knew deep down that Bashkim would never see things from her perspective. He would never believe that she never intended to harm anyone, that she loved her country and its people just as much as he did. In her heart of hearts, she knew that she could never convince him of that considering what she had done.

Her secret threatened to smash her but she also knew that this heavy weight was only for her to bear. It wasn't the type of problem that anyone would want to help her with. Tears fell from her eyes and she gently wiped them away, determined to find a solution for whatever assignment they asked of her this time and hopefully be done with it quickly. With a deep breath, she reassured herself that she would indeed figure something out. Despite the unsettling feeling in her gut, she hoped that the message left for her wouldn't be too urgent. Maybe it was nothing to worry about, she told herself. But as she glanced down at her phone, she couldn't shake the nagging thought that this was something different and a bigger assignment than the previous ones.

A prominent socialite, she understood the importance of presenting herself in the best light at all times and with tonight's grand event, she had the perfect opportunity to do just that. She meticulously picked every little detail of her outfit dripping with lavish jewellery, determined to exude the very essence of elegance and sophistication. As she made her way out of the house, she thought of the influential guests who would be also attending the party, many of whom were her former classmates turned powerful figures in Government and other areas of public life. It was crucial for her to stay relevant, not just for the sake of her luxurious lifestyle, but also so that she and her children could be safe! She even contemplated leaving her old phone at home, but the fear of missing an important call forced her to tuck it into her small evening bag. What if they came to her house looking for her? The thought alone made her shudder and she quickly pushed it to the back of her mind.

Before heading to the door she made arrangements for her children and their caregiver, ensuring that everything would be in order during her absence. She called for a taxi and, in a calm and measured tone, gave the nanny explicit instructions on what the children would eat for dinner, what time they should go to bed, and which bedtime stories should be read to them. She tenderly hugged her children, enveloping them in a warm embrace and expressing her love for them in a soft and reassuring voice. As she turned to leave, she cast a final, lingering glance at them, a feeling of apprehension swirling within her. The thought of the ominous message and everything that could unravel lingered at the edge of her consciousness, but she did her best to push it aside and focus on the present. What she hoped for was a thrilling evening with her friends.

Besa stepped out of the taxi, her eyes scanning the surroundings, searching for Ariana. And there she was, standing in the corner of the building, a vision in red, her thick, flowy black hair cascading down her back like a waterfall. Without hesitation, Besa waved at Ariana, her excitement visible, her heart pounding in her chest. As Ariana rushed to meet her, they fell into each other's arms, their embrace conveying all the words that remained unspoken. They held each other tightly, rocking side to side, lost in the joy of reunion.

"Don't cry!" Ariana told her, though tears were filling both their eyes, a testament to the depth of their emotions. "You're making us both ruin our makeup."Ariana said, pulling back to look at her friend. "I can't believe you're finally here," "Let me look at you! You haven't changed a bit!"

"And you," Besa replied, her voice choked with emotion, "you got younger with age. You look gorgeous. I missed you so much!" Her tears clouded her vision, and she gratefully accepted the tissue Ariana offered her.

"I'm so happy to see you," Ariana said.

As Besa and Ariana attempted to compose themselves, wiping away their tears with delicate care, the crowd around them began to grow. Well-wishers and old friends stopped to greet them, smiles of joy spreading across their faces as they embraced one another warmly. The air was filled with the sound of laughter and chatter, and the energy of the moment was electric. The music could now be heard in the banqueting hall , prompting the excited crowd of people to join in. Besa's heart was pounding with a mix of emotions, her body trembling with the thrill of being amongst people who had known her intimately, who recognized her face and knew her name. It was a feeling that she had missed, the warmth of being surrounded by friends. In that moment, Besa felt like a teenager again, caught up in the rush of life.

As Besa and Ariana crossed the threshold into the grand hall, Besa again felt a surge of emotion welling up inside of her. For years, she had dreamed of being here, amongst the people with whom she had shared so many formative experiences. They were the ones with whom she had spent countless hours in classrooms, exploring the world of knowledge and learning together. The sense of community that pervaded the air was palpable, as if the walls themselves were alive like giant silver screens playing all the memories and shared experiences. The bonds of friendship that had been forged such a long time ago seemed to have passed the test of time. In this city, people knew each other's life stories, each other's parents, siblings, apartments where each had lived, the playgrounds where they played, the cafes where they met . If the war hadn't ravaged their country, these people would have been able to maintain their friendships for life. People rarely moved away from their hometown and even when they did, there was always a family member or a friend of a friend that kept it all going. The ties that bound them were solid, forged through shared history that was both joyous and painful.

After a very long time Besa felt warmth rushing through her. The bond that she had with these people was not easy to explain to an outsider. It somehow felt primordial.

As she looked around the room, she recognized faces from her past, and her heart swelled with joy and gratitude. The sense of belonging that she had missed so much seemed to be coming back. She was overwhelmed by emotions, and tears welled in her eyes, mingling with laughter. She looked carefully at each person, trying to match faces to names, to recollect the moments they had shared together. She hugged everyone that approached her perhaps for a little bit longer than necessary, unwilling to let go of the warmth and happiness they brought her. She couldn't remember the last time she felt this happy, this alive.

As they weaved through the throngs of people, Ariana, on the other hand, felt a sense of unease in her stomach. She had spent years avoiding this crowd, carefully steering clear of those she had once called friends. But now, she was making small talk and pretending to be thrilled to see them all. Despite her discomfort, she stood patiently beside Besa as she introduced her to one person after another. The familiar faces blurred together, and Ariana struggled to keep up with the names and stories that Besa shared. Finally, when she felt like she had endured enough, Ariana made her excuses and slipped away from the crowd, leaving Besa to hold court in the hall's foyer. As she made her way through the crowd, the knot in her stomach tightened. Each step felt like a marathon. The sound of her heels echoed in her ears, a stark contrast to the festive music of the celebration. She could sense the eyes of the people in the room following her every move, dissecting her like a specimen on display. She began to regret her choice of dress, the bold red fabric now drawing unwanted attention. The burden of keeping her cool and to continue smiling started to weigh on her. The faces of Arben's old friends came into focus. She wondered what they might be whispering about, and whether they knew about her struggles. Tears threatened to spill from her eyes, but she held them back with all her strength.

As Ariana approached her assigned table, she noticed Fatime's familiar face. The years had been kind to her friend, she thought. Fatime still looked like a teenager, her eyes still sparkled with warmth and her smile lit up her entire face when she saw Ariana. Fatime looked elegant and comfortable in her modest dress and low heels. "She looks exactly as she did in High School," Ariana thought.

"She's always been the sensible one," Ariana mused inwardly, "while I'm here looking like a hot mess." Seeing Fatime after all these years brought a warm smile to Ariana's face, easing her discomfort.

Without hesitation, Fatime jumped up from her seat and wrapped up Ariana in a warm embrace. They started talking, delving deep into memories of their high school days. It was as if they had just stepped out of class into recess in their high school yard. Ariana fondly recalled how Fatime had helped her countless times with class work, tests, and homework during their time as classmates. She was overjoyed to see her.

 "Oh my god, you look the same as you did 20 years ago" Ariana told her.

"Maybe it's the dress," Fatime laughed. "This is the dress I was supposed to wear to the prom. We went together to buy it, remember?"

"Really? I don't remember a thing." Ariana admitted, laughing.

Fatime smiled, her eyes twinkling "We were so excited about the prom. We spent hours at that little shop and ended up skipping class and got in trouble."

Ariana's eyes widened in surprise "I can't believe you remember all that. My memory is so hazy." They continued reminiscing, their conversation flowing effortlessly. The years melted away, and for that moment, they reconnected again as if no time had passed at all.

Ariana, who hadn't talked so much to anyone in ages, found herself trying to concentrate on her conversation with Fatime, but the pounding in her head seemed to grow louder. She struggled to hear her friend's words over the noise of the crowd, the music, and the chattering all around them and her mind kept drifting away. She had forgotten about the day spent with Fatime at the little shop twenty years ago, but now she remembered that after school that day, Arben and she had met and spent hours kissing passionately, talking and laughing while hiding in the little garden behind the shop. Everything tonight was going to remind her of him. How was she going to survive the evening?

" So much noise!"Ariana said, looking up just in time to see Besa approaching the table together with Suzi.

"Look who I found" Besa exclaimed jubilantly "Suzi hasn't changed a bit" "I can't believe it, she even looks younger. How can that be possible?"

"It's called Botox," Ariana muttered cynically into Fatime's ear, who smiled widely and jumped up to greet and hug Besa and Suzi.

"Fatime!" exclaimed Besa, hugging her, "I can't believe it's you! You look wonderful"

"You too!" said Fatime holding back tears. "I'm so, so happy to see you!"

"Hi Ariana" said Suzi, extending her beautifully manicured hand adorned with gold rings, "Long time no see. Where have you been hiding?"

"Hi," said Ariana with a slight grin "I've been working like crazy, no time to see anyone". They did the customary cheek kiss, careful not to mess up each other's make-up. As they settled back into their seats, the conversation flowed easily, though Ariana's mind continued to wander. She couldn't shake the pounding in her head.

Besa, back to being a social butterfly that she was in high school, launched into a series of updates about her life, drawing laughter and gasps from the group. Suzi, with her perfectly styled hair and flawless skin, chimed in with her own tales, each one more glamorous than the last. Fatime, always the supportive friend, listened intently, her eyes shining with genuine interest. Ariana, on the other hand, struggled to stay engaged.

The Hall was filled with people still arriving at the party. Music blasted from huge speakers, and the crowd moved about, waving, shaking hands, and hugging each other. Ariana fidgeted with her necklace and constantly tugged at the neckline of her dress, hoping to conceal more of her skin. Suzi's sharp eyes immediately caught Ariana's unease during their exchanged pleasantries. She attempted to engage Ariana in conversation, asking about her job and how she was faring, but Ariana seemed distant, avoiding direct eye contact.

A strange feeling gnawed at Suzi. Something didn't feel right. She couldn't figure out why Ariana was behaving so coldly. She wasn't even asking about Suzi's children, a usual topic between them. Suzi probed, asking about how things were at the office and how she and Bashkim were getting along after what Suzi called the friendship between the three of them, hit a rough patch.

Then it hit her! In a split second, while she tried to catch Ariana's gaze without success and as Ariana mumbled, trying to change the subject or ignore her, Suzi realised the truth: Ariana was with Bashkim. Her stomach churned with a mix of anger and betrayal. She glanced around the room, trying to mask her shock and maintain her composure. The music, the laughter, the chatter—all of it seemed to fade into the background. Ariana, still fidgeting, seemed oblivious to Suzi's realisation. She continued to tug at her dress, her discomfort now starkly apparent. Suzi took a deep breath, forcing a smile as she decided to confront Ariana later, away from the prying eyes and ears of the party. For now, she nodded along to the conversation, her mind already crafting the questions she needed answers to. The party continued to swirl around them, but for Suzi, the night had taken a drastically different turn. Losing a husband to some strange woman didn't feel as bad as losing him to a friend. Ariana was her friend, for God's sake. How could she take Bashkim's side, or worse, be his lover? Suzi thought. She became livid, and as she sat in her chair, trying to pay attention to the conversations between the women, the room seemed to spin around her. She was overwhelmed with emotion, feeling as though she had been hit by a bus. She never saw this coming and felt blindsided. The sense of betrayal cut to the core of her being. She fought to maintain her composure, but it was a losing battle. Her forced smile faltered as she struggled to keep pretending everything was fine. She tried to keep her attention away from Ariana for the rest of the evening, focusing on anything and everything else. The pain in her chest and jaw remained, a constant reminder of the knife that seemed to have lodged itself in her back. Desperate for relief, she called for a cocktail, feeling the need to numb the pain.

The evening was moving along very quickly. Drinks were being poured and food was being served. People were talking, laughing and dancing *valle* in circles holding each other's hands up as they moved three steps forward and one backwards as people in these parts had done for thousands of years! People moved from table to table, greeting and hugging each other, doing the rounds around the hall for the second or third time to ensure they hadn't missed anyone. The atmosphere was charged with a mix of excitement and nostalgia. Conversations flowed freely, covering topics of life, families, and work. Inevitably, the talk often turned to the past— who had been lost in the war, how people had survived, and how they were coping now. Tears of sadness and joy mingled as stories were shared. One corner of the room might echo with laughter, where old friends reminisced about their youthful escapades, while another corner saw quiet, heartfelt conversations about loved ones who were no longer there.

Besa's heart was overflowing with joy as she moved gracefully from table to table, greeting old friends and new acquaintances alike. She was radiant, her infectious smile lighting up the entire room. As the music swelled and the crowd continued to dance, she joined in without hesitation, taking her place in the line of dancers and moving to the beat with effortless grace. The steps were familiar, ingrained in her since childhood when she had eagerly danced at weddings and celebrations of her large family. She sang along with the singers as she remembered the words to almost all the folk songs too. Lost in the moment she felt completely at ease. This was where she belonged and now she was sure that her decision to come back was the right one. As she twirled and stepped, she caught glimpses of familiar faces in the crowd—faces that had aged, yet carried the same essence of the young people she had known so well. There were smiles of recognition, waves of acknowledgment, and even a few tears of joy. Each interaction reaffirmed her sense of belonging, her connection to this place and these people. For Besa, there was no better feeling in the world.

Ariana sat still, her body almost frozen in place except for the subtle rise and fall of her chest. Her eyes were fixed on an imaginary point in the distance, lost in thought. She only stood up to slip outside into the cool night air for a cigarette or to disappear into the bathroom to check her makeup and whisper words of self-encouragement to herself in the mirror. Despite herself, Ariana's eyes kept straying towards Arben's friends. She knew she shouldn't look at them, shouldn't seek to see Arben amongst them, but she couldn't help it. One of the men had been a close friend to both her and Arben, a witness to their hurried wedding ceremony in the town hall. Yet, he hadn't approached her to say hello. She wondered why. Should she be the one to initiate the conversation? Could she find the courage to do that without bursting into tears? Her mind was a jumble of thoughts, each one more painful than the last. She asked herself why she was torturing herself like this, why she couldn't just go home. Suzi's sudden coldness and provocation only added to her misery. Ariana knew that Suzi had figured out that she and Bashkim were together, and it made her hate herself even more. She didn't know what to say to her. She was afraid to even look at her in the face. She continued to top her glass of wine as she sat next to Fatime, who also remained still, lost in her own thoughts. Ariana's eyes kept darting around the room, searching for Arben's face. It was as if she was hoping against hope that Arben would appear, surrounded by his friends, his eyes sparkling and his smile warm. Watching his friends laughing, Ariana's heart ached with the memory of Arben's laugh. She thought she could almost hear it again, a warm pleasant laughter that had filled her heart with joy. She felt as though his spirit was present in the hall, as he was watching her. The pain of his absence was making her heart ache and restricted her breathing. She felt as if she couldn't get enough air.

Fatime sat in her chair, trying to keep her body still, but she couldn't stop fidgeting. Her fingers played nervously with a strand of hair. At one moment, she felt as though she was in a dream, as if she would wake up any second and find herself in her bedroom. And then a strange fear would creep in, a fear of Agim storming in and dragging her out of there in front of everyone. Her heart jumped like a caged bird in her chest, so she ate to distract herself, and talked and talked to anyone who would listen. It was as if a dam had burst inside her, and a flood of words just spilled out uncontrollably. Fatime realised that she hadn't talked this much since high school, and in fact, there had been days, weeks, even months when she had barely spoken a word to anyone. She had thought she had forgotten how to hold a conversation, but tonight, the words flowed like a swollen river after a heavy storm. She spoke with Ariana, with Suzi, with Besa, and with many other friends who stopped by to greet her. And for a moment, just a moment, she forgot about the fear that had been haunting her about coming here tonight.

She found herself weaving a web of stories about her absent husband when they asked why he wasn't here tonight.She told her friends a lie that Agim had stayed behind to care for his sick mother and had urged her to come to the party and enjoy herself in his absence. She also told them the truth of her recent online accounting degree, and the job waiting for her in Sarandë, Albania, where she would be heading first thing in the morning. When she said this out loud, she could hardly believe it herself. She then lied again and told them that Agim would be joining her in Sarande, once she had settled in. Fatime spoke of Agim's successful supermarket business, and how they were planning to open a new store in Sarandë. She smiled to herself at the thought of this. How she had hoped till just this morning that Agim would all of a sudden become his old self. That he would wake up this morning and hug her and tell her sorry for everything and listen to her plans for them. How they would just come here tonight together and then leave together for Sarande, holding hands, dancing and being in love the same way as when they fell in love at the other high school party years ago.

Fatime took another sip of her drink, trying to push the thoughts away, and continued to spin her tales. She dreamed of living by the sea, she admitted to her friends, and that much was true. She also felt a pang of guilt and regret for the man she was leaving behind, but she didn't say that to her friends. The guilt and doubts crept in, making her question whether she had done enough to save their marriage. Was she being cruel for leaving him? These thoughts tortured her, as she still couldn't tell the whole truth to her friends who showered her with encouragement and praise, assuring her that she was making the right move and would thrive in Sarande.

"Saranda is a beautiful town," Suzi told her.

"I have a summer house there which unfortunately I can't visit much"

"Why don't I give you my housekeeper's phone number there and you can go and stay in my villa for as long as you like" Suzi told her.

"What? For real?" Fatimja couldn't believe her luck. She was so happy she could scream.

"Are you sure?" She kept asking Suzi "I don't want to impose" she said again.

"Oh please!" Said Suzi "I insist!" and got her phone out and shared the number of her housekeeper, her address and all the information that Fatime would need. "I will text her right now to tell her you will be there tomorrow."

Suzi's offer felt unbelievable, like winning a lottery, warming Fatime's heart and lifting her spirits. Her dear friend's words transported her to the enchanting town of Saranda already, where she could see herself soaking up the sun, listening to the sound of the waves, and breathing in the salty sea air. The kindness of her friends made her feel like she was part of a loving community once more and for the first time in a long while she didn't feel alone. These women, her dear friends, that didn't really know anything about her life struggles yet, were unknowingly saving her. They were unknowingly undoing all the pain and suffering that she had endured all these years. Her confidence was growing by the minute. Her fear was diminishing with every word and every praise that they were saying to her. She was remembering who she was and she felt like she was becoming her old self.

She thought about the new life that was awaiting her as she touched her duffel bag under the table with her feet, to make sure it was still there and that she was leaving for Sarande for real. As she tapped the hard metal of the gun with her foot, she thought it was probably a mistake to have taken the gun from the living room closet. She pushed the bag a few more inches further under the table, making sure the girls wouldn't see it.

When she decided to leave for Sarande and started packing her things, she remembered the gun her father-in-law had bought when Agim was in prison. He had hidden it in the top cabinet in the living room. "In case you ever need it, it's right here. If the police decide to come into the house, at least you can protect yourself." he had told her. Agim never knew about the gun's existence. Fatime had forgotten about it but at the last minute, after packing her bag, she remembered. The thought of living alone for the first time made her uneasy, and having the gun would make her feel safer. After her father in law passed away, she was the only one who knew about the weapon in the house. She didn't know how to use it, but she knew it was loaded and figured she would figure it out if she ever needed to. Generally, she was good with every type of machinery or appliance she'd had to use.

Her smile, once forced and hollow, now radiated a joy that came naturally. For the first time in what felt like ages, she felt unburdened, liberated - like a bird finally freed from its cage.

As she basked in the warmth of her friends' company, Fatime felt a sense of awakening stir within her. This was who she was, the person she had forgotten during long years of hardship. As the music swelled and the energy in the room rose, she found herself rising to her feet. Tentatively at first, but then with growing confidence, she began to weave her way through the crowd, determined not to miss to greet a single soul. She asked Ariana if she wanted to go with her to meet and greet other people.

"I'm ok" said Ariana," you go ahead "I might go outside and light another cigarette but for now I'll stay here."

Ariana, still feeling the effects of the wine, watched as Fatime left the table, her steps light and graceful. It was then that she heard it - a faint buzzing, coming from somewhere near her. She looked at the phones on the table, but none of them were the source of the sound. Curiosity getting the better of her, Ariana checked her own phone, only to find that it wasn't buzzing either. Puzzled, she scanned the room, her eyes lingering on the dancers in the centre. But the buzzing persisted, a persistent hum that seemed to grow louder by the second. Ariana's gaze drifted to the table and the empty chairs where the ladies were sitting a few minutes ago, then she looked under the table. She saw Fatime's duffel bag. She was puzzled. The ringtone that she was hearing was strange, unlike any she had heard on the new phones. It was an old-fashioned sound, reminiscent of old cell phones. Desperate to find her friends and solve the mystery of the buzzing phone, Ariana scanned the room once more, her head still hurting. She couldn't see any of them. She crouched beneath the table, her eyes fixed on the duffel bag. Slowly, she opened it and reached inside, her hand searching blindly for any object that might be making the buzzing noise.

Her fingers brushed against cold metal, and she pulled back her hand in shock. A gun? This wasn't what she had been expecting at all. Her mind raced as she tried to make sense of what she had discovered. The duffle bag was close to Fatime's chair and she had noticed that Fatime had reached out to glance under there several times during the evening. Why would Fatime, of all people, be carrying a gun? The bag was full of clothes. Fatime had said that she was going to Sarande after the party but Ariana didn't know that she had meant that quite literally.

Shaken, she quickly closed the zipper of tha bag and sat back straight on her chair, her thoughts in turmoil. The buzzing of the phone only added to her unease. As she looked around the hall, searching for the other women and not being able to find them with her eyes, the crowded room had suddenly become claustrophobic, closing in on her from all sides. She tried to ignore the buzzing of the phone, telling herself that it was probably all in her head or her ears were buzzing from the noise and the music. The buzzing would stop for a few seconds and then start again. Looking again on the chairs and on the table and under it, she finally pinpointed where the phone buzzing was coming from. She nervously reached for Suzi's small, Chanel bag. The incessant buzzing had become unbearable, and she knew that she needed to find the phone and put an end to the noise that was driving her crazy. Her eyes roamed the room once more in search of Suzi. She couldn't see her.

Annoyed, she let out a deep sigh and she reached inside the bag and finally, she felt the small phone vibrating in her hand. It was Suzi's Nokia, an old model that seemed out of place in her expensive designer handbag. Why would someone like Suzi, who had all the latest gadgets and technology, still be using such an outdated phone? And why was it buzzing so insistently? It was driving her crazy.

For a moment, she considered leaving the phone where it was and simply telling Suzi about the call later. But then she thought, what if something happened to her children? This made her quickly reconsider. With a sense of urgency, Ariana rose from her seat and began scanning the room for Suzi, the buzzing phone still gripped tightly in her hand. She couldn't take that noise anymore, so she flipped the phone open, covered her mouth with her hand to muffle the sound and said "Allo" while walking out of the venue and into the hallway to hear better. She was about to ask if she could take a message for Suzi, who wasn't available right now, but the deep, angry voice didn't give her a chance to speak. He kept ranting. She froze completely on hearing more clearly the voice coming through the line. The man spoke in Serbian. It felt strangely familiar.

"Where the hell are you? I've left you hundreds of messages!" the deep male voice shouted in Serbian. Ariana's mind went into overdrive as she tried to process what she was hearing. She hadn't heard Serbian spoken in many years, except in her nightmares. Her heart started to beat faster, her blood boiling. Her face turned red and she began to feel dizzy. She wanted to ask in Serbian if she could take a message for Suzi because she wasn't available, but the words wouldn't come out. She just couldn't speak that language anymore.

Instead, she said "Da" ("Yes") in Serbian, not quite knowing why.

"Slušaj", "Listen" the voice said "You have to come tonight and meet me in Gracanica" The voice continued, giving her precise instructions about where to go. The urgency in his tone made it clear that this was very serious, possibly a matter of life and death.

"It's very important," the voice insisted, "I'll wait for you. I can't leave until I see you. I have to give you something"

Ariana said "Da" again, feeling a growing lump in her throat, her eyes welling up with tears.

She knew she had heard that voice before. She recognized the harshness, the smoker's rasp. She felt lightheaded. Was she imagining everything? Was she having a nightmare? The face that matched that ugly voice floated in her memory, but she couldn't be sure. Just before hanging up, the man on the phone said a phrase that had echoed in Ariana's consciousness all these years, a phrase she couldn't shake since that cold April day in '99.

Ariana felt cold shivers run down her spine, her whole body shivering as she searched for a seat in the foyer. "Sweetheart, don't upset me! I can be a real gentleman, but don't push your luck!" the voice said in a hoarse, raspy tone.

She closed her eyes in disbelief, and in a flash, she was back in the barn next to the road where her life had changed forever. Her head was spinning, replaying the traumatic events she had tried to forget for twenty years. Her body trembled as she fought to keep her cool. The man's voice on the phone, speaking in Serbian, had triggered a storm of emotions she thought she had managed to bury. She had spent years trying to forget the horrors she had endured, but now they all came back in a crushing wave. She remembered clearly those exact words spoken to her by a paramilitary soldier as he prepared to assault her.

Tears started rolling down her cheeks. She whispered a final "Da" and closed the phone.

She wiped her tears and looked around, feeling disoriented. The music and chatter from the party behind the big closed door of the hall seemed distant as she tried to stop her body from shaking. Her mind reeled from the phone call as she struggled to compose herself. Slowly, she reentered the hall, her brain foggy. She carefully put the small phone back in Suzi's bag, ensuring it went unnoticed, and took a sip of water to calm her nerves. She looked around the room to see if anyone had noticed her distress. Sweat beaded on her forehead, and her heart raced in a state of panic. A waiter approached her table, asking if she needed another glass of wine. She didn't reply. Ariana's hands were still shaking, threatening to spill the water onto the floor. She struggled to keep her composure, taking deep breaths, as discreetly as possible.

Without waiting to see if any of her friends were coming back to the table, Ariana grabbed her cigarettes and headed out to get some air. As she stood outside, taking another drag, her thoughts spiralled out of control. The cool night air did nothing to calm her racing mind. She couldn't shake off her horror.

"What just happened?" she kept asking herself. "What the f... just happened?" she whispered, the smoke from her cigarette trailing up into the night sky.

"I'm not that drunk! What happened just now is not a dream!" She tried to make sense of everything. Was she losing her mind? Was the emotional stress of tonight too much for her, meaning she finally snapped? Should she call Bashkim and tell him what had just happened?

She hesitated. What if he was a part of this? What if he and Suzi were a team, spies working together for the Serbs? As the minister of the interior, having access to all the security information and not knowing that your wife is a spy seemed doubtful. She pictured Bashkim's face, trying to think if there was ever an instance where he might have behaved suspiciously in any way. She couldn't think of any such instance.

Ariana took a deep drag on her cigarette and exhaled slowly, trying to calm her racing thoughts. She knew she needed to take action without delay.

For twenty years, Ariana had longed for the chance to avenge the trauma inflicted upon her. She had worked tirelessly to rise through the ranks of the Ministry of the Interior, all with the hope of one day bringing the perpetrators of the atrocities to justice. She had even secretly dreamed of a moment to be face to face with her rapist, if not in court, then to execute raw revenge - not just for herself but for all the innocent civilians who suffered and lost their lives for no other reason except that they were of the 'wrong' ethnicity.

And now, the man she had been searching for all these years had just given her the opportunity to finally confront him.

As she stood there, smoking her cigarette, trying to get her thoughts in order, doubts and questions raced through her mind. What was the right course of action? Should she seize the opportunity for revenge or let the past rest, as she had been advised to do all these years? Should she ignore the fact that she could finally do what she had dreamed of for so long? Was the desire for revenge too primitive, too primal? Should she rise above it? One thing she couldn't ignore was the feeling of seething anger that gripped her, the same anger that had fuelled her survival for so many years. It appears that the universe has answered to grant her unconscious wish, the opportunity for revenge unlike any she had ever dared to admit dreaming of.

This is a chance for her to confront her attacker on her own terms, to take control of her own destiny, she thought. She knew, without a shadow of a doubt, that this man was responsible for killing Arben and for causing her the trauma that had haunted her and she didn't need any judge or jury to confirm that. Was she going to take matters into her own hands or was she going to wait forever for some strangers to come to conclusions that she already knew? In this moment, the Universe also granted her a sense of clarity and purpose. She felt simmering rage within her, a desire for justice that burned like wildfire.

She gazed up at the sky and for the first time in her life she felt a connection to something greater than herself. The sun had already sunk below the horizon, the sky was transformed into a canvas of deep blues and purples, and the gentle glow of the moon and the stars began to fill the night sky. Not a single cloud could be seen on that beautiful summer evening, as if the heavens themselves were offering a perfect stage for the scene that was unfolding.

She took a deep breath once again and her thoughts turned to Arben, whom she had loved and lost forever but in that moment she felt like he was there with her, his spirit hovering in the air, a comforting presence that she could feel with every fibre of her being.

She took her time, letting her thoughts settle and her emotions calm. This was not a situation to be taken lightly, and she needed to think carefully about what to do next.

As she lit another cigarette, her mind was made up. She knew exactly what she was going to do. She would not call the police, and she would not have them arrest Suzi, no matter what. Instead, she would give her a chance to explain herself, to tell her side of the story. She needed to know what was going on. With her thoughts organised and her intentions clear, she repeated to herself the words and instructions that she had received from the person on the phone. She knew that this was not going to be easy, but she was ready for whatever lay ahead.

She made her way back into the hall, her footsteps lighter and more confident. She headed for the bathroom, where she took a moment to fix her makeup and apply a fresh coat of red lipstick. As she looked at herself in the mirror, she gazed deep into her own eyes and forced herself to smile. She found a long time ago that forcing a smile gave her an instant mood boost and confidence.

"You can do this," she whispered to herself, and with that, she left the bathroom, her posture now straighter and more poised than before. As she walked towards her table, she was met with the familiar face of Besa. "Where were you?" Besa asked her, her voice laced with concern. "You stayed outside longer than you were here! You should stop smoking; you're missing all the fun." Ariana smiled, feeling a sense of warmth and affection for her friend. "Don't worry about me," she reassured her. "You're the one who should be having fun. I can't believe you came all the way from the US just to see these people and dance to this appalling music. And I thought you were cool," Ariana teased, her laughter now coming out of her with ease. Besa chuckled, happy to see her friend in a better mood. "You looked so gloomy and upset all night," she remarked, taking a seat next to Ariana. "Are you sure you're okay?" "I'm fine," Ariana said, giving Besa a reassuring smile. "You go ahead and dance." Besa nodded, standing up to join the exuberant line of dancers again as an upbeat song began to play. As Besa moved towards the centre of the crowd, Ariana sat back, contemplating the next moves. She looked around more intently in order to find Suzi in the crowd. It wasn't long before she spotted her at the bar, her Chanel bag slung over her shoulder like a badge of loftiness. Ariana's heart quickened with anticipation and apprehension. She tried to sense any sign of tension or anxiety in Suzi's face. Wasn't she meant to be in some dark basement in Gracanica, receiving instructions? Even though she didn't get that phone call, there were tens of missed calls and voice messages that she must have seen by now. Instead Suzana was still there, sipping her drink? Without a second thought, Ariana leaned under the table and unzipped Fatime's duffel bag, her fingers curling around the cold metal of Fatime's gun. It was a risk, but a necessary one. She carefully placed the weapon in her own bag and closed it. Rising to her feet, Ariana made her way towards the bar, her gaze fixed on Suzana.

Their eyes met for the first time that evening, and Ariana felt a flicker of adrenaline rushing through her veins. She leaned to get closer to Suzana, her lips brushing against her ear.

"Can we talk outside please? Me and you," she said quietly in her ear, conveying a whispered order. Suzana's surprise was evident in her expression, but Ariana pressed on, her voice low and insistent. "Now!" She told her, "It's important."

Suzana hesitated for a moment, her hand hovering over her drink, before finally nodding her agreement. "Yes sure, I can talk for a few minutes, because I have to leave. I was just going to have one more drink." Ariana's response was firm and immediate. "Leave the drink!" she commanded. Ariana gently took Suzi's elbow and led her through the bustling crowd, their steps unhurried and deliberate. As they emerged from the venue, the night air greeted them with a cool embrace, and they made their way to the edge of the building, in the parking lot, away from the noise and the lights. Without a word, Ariana pulled out her pack of cigarettes and offered one to Suzi, her own fingers deftly working to light up. She scanned the area, making sure that no prying eyes or ears were nearby.

Suzi's voice broke the silence as Ariana faced her, her gaze steady and unwavering.

"I know there's something going on between you and Bahkim, and I don't care," Suzi said, her words measured and calm. "If that's what you wanted to talk to me about, then I don't think there's much we could say to each other."

Ariana seemed unmoved by this comment. "It's not about that," she said, her voice low and urgent. "There's something else, something much more important." Suzi braced herself for what Ariana was going to say, anticipating Ariana's fiery temper to flare up and explode in a raging inferno. Her heart hammered in her chest as she was afraid of Ariana's mood. She prepared to apologise to her just so she could end this conversation and get it over with before Ariana's temper exploded. But Ariana surprised her with her restrained anger. She was maintaining her composure even though her fury was evident. With a look of intense anger etched on her face, she nevertheless spoke softly, almost in a whisper.

"Yes, I know that you know," she said, her cheeks burning a bright red. "And it's true, me and Bashkim have been together for a few months now. But that's not what I want to talk to you about." Now, Suzi felt her anger begin to simmer, threatening to boil over at any moment. How could Ariana be so brazen, so shameless? she thought. Not only was she dating her husband and destroyed the friendship between them, but now she was dismissing everything as if it were a trivial matter.

"I don't think there's anything that me and you can discuss about anymore" Suzi said as she threw her cigarette on the ground and stepped on it with the tip of her sandals.

"Yes, we have actually" Ariana said and reached and grabbed her elbow again.

"I picked up your phone about fifteen minutes ago and I found out something that I'm sure you don't want anyone else to know about."

Suzi's heart began to race as she tried to process Ariana's words. She couldn't believe what she was hearing - how could Ariana have picked up her phone without her noticing?

"What? Suzi asked while she turned pale in a way that even her makeup couldn't mask.

"What phone? I don't know what you're talking about plus why on earth do you pick up other people's phones? Are you that drunk already? Have you lost your mind? What are you talking about?" she asked again being visibly shaken and furious at Ariana

"Shhhhh... " Ariana told her. "Keep your voice down. You don't want to cause a scene or have me call the police right now and have them ask you questions instead,"

Ariana's grip on her elbow tightened, and she leaned in close. "I found out about your little secret," she hissed in Suzana's ear. " A secret that could destroy your entire life if it ever got out." Suzi felt a wave of panic wash over her. She knew exactly what Ariana was talking about.

"I don't know what you're talking about," Suzi said, her voice shaking. "Please, just let me go. I don't want any trouble." Ariana released her grip on Suzi's elbow, but she didn't move away. Instead, she stood there, staring at Suzi with a look of cold determination in her eyes. "You're not going anywhere," Ariana said. "Not until you talk to me about this. And trust me, I'm the only one that could help you and believe it or not I'm on your side. I want to protect you". "The Nokia phone that you had in your evening bag was buzzing like crazy non-stop while you were dancing or talking to people at the bar." Ariana continued still whispering with urgency in her voice. "It was going on and on I was afraid that something might have happened to your children. I picked up the phone after I couldn't see you anywhere." Ariana said.

Suzi stood there frozen and terrified.

"The man at the other end of the line started talking because he was upset and didn't wait for me to tell him that I'm just a worried friend who wanted to take a message.... and let me tell you,... I'm so glad that I did pick up that phone call." Ariana was fuming with anger at this point but was still trying hard to not raise her voice.

Her voice trembled as she struggled to keep it in a whisper, her heart pounding with so many emotions. With trembling fingers, she clutched the gun in her bag, dreading the next words that would spill out of her mouth as she had to finally tell Suzi about her abuse during the war.

"The person you work for," she breathed out, her words heavy with pain and agony. "They not only want to see you tonight, but they also have specific instructions to harm this tortured country.." she paused and took a deep breath "After listening to his voice, I am positive that he is the same man who raped me and killed Arben." she finally said.

Suzi's eyes filled with tears as she clutched her hand over her mouth, disbelief etched across her face. She was shocked! The weight of Ariana's words hung heavy in the air, suffocating Suzi with their enormity. She wasn't sure what to say. Her stomach was turning upside down. She had known to an extent who those people that gave her orders and assignments on the phone were, but she could have never imagined that they were the same ones that had committed crimes during the war here. She felt so guilty, so sorry. She didn't know what to say.

"Please listen to me" Suzi pleaded, desperation colouring her voice. "They threatened me with my kids, and they're holding my brother in prison somewhere in Serbia. They keep telling me that only I can save him. They told me they would kill or take away Rron from me if I didn't cooperate." Suzi was now wailing softly. She looked broken.

Ariana's heart sank as she listened to Suzi's tale of woe, trying to calm her down with a shushing motion. She could only imagine what that guy would be able to do to Suzi and her children. "Please, Ariana" Suzi whispered, her eyes scanning the area. "You have to believe me. I have never given them any valuable information. I was meaning to tell Bashkim everything for so long now, but I was too afraid. One of the reasons that I wanted Bashkim out of the house was to not have him implicated in this or not have him find out.

I was afraid, if I told him anything he would be the one to throw me in jail and take my children away. There was no way out for me."

Suzi's tears rolled down her face as she implored Ariana to trust her, to believe her.

Ariana took a deep breath as she thought of Suzi's children, of Rron and how much he struggled with autism. How much Ariana loved him. His treatments in Belgrade were helping him a lot.

"Is Bashkim in this too?" Ariana asked Suzi apprehensively, hoping for her to confirm what she said before that Bashkim didn't know anything about this.

"No, no of course he is not" "He will kill me when he finds out!" Suzi was now walking in small circles and moving left and right whimpering and holding her mouth to stop herself from crying too loud.

"Please, please don't tell him!" she was pleading to Ariana.

"Under one condition" Ariana said, interrupting her.

"I want you to call that man right now and tell him that you will meet him in 30 minutes.'

Suzi was looking at her puzzled.

"You want me to meet him? Will the police follow me and catch him? I should at least get a pardon when they catch him, shouldn't I ? Suzi asked, seeing how her situation could turn around, from traitor to hero.

"No," said Ariana, " There will be no police involved. Yet. I want you to meet him and I'm coming with you. We'll listen to exactly what he wants. We will call the police after. Call him now and tell him you're on your way!."

This wasn't making sense to Suzi.

"Why should we risk our lives?" She said in a calmer whisper now.

"Plus I don't even have my car here. I came in a taxi. Let's just call the police and let them deal with him."

"No, no," Ariana said, "I want to deal with him first!"

"Call him! Now!" She ordered Suzi.

She looked at Suzi sternly and Suzi knew not to say anything when faced with that look.

"Please," she whispered, " Think about the children. I'm your friend for God's sake."

Ariana just looked at her blankly pointing towards Suzi's bag where her phone was.

"Call him!" She said one more time.

"Hallo" Suzi was talking on the phone now.

"I'll be there in 30 minutes". She told the guy in Serbian

"I'm still waiting" the guy said "Hurry up!"

A rush of adrenaline swept through them as they sprinted towards Ariana's car, their hearts pounding in their chests. Without hesitation, Ariana slipped into the backseat, her voice calm but urgent as she commanded, "You drive."

Their destination was Gracanica, a Serb enclave, about 30-minutes' drive from the city. A community of 10,000 people lived there and they were mostly ethnic Serbs. The tiny village with its big Orthodox Monastery church and small houses with little vegetable gardens, its narrow and badly asphalted streets, and few dim lights looked like a time travelling portal to ex-Yugoslavia; Time in that village had stood in 1990 or thereabouts! Same houses, same fences, same roofs.

Ariana lay in the back seat of the car. She had a large blanket she always kept on the back seat of her car for when she took her cat on outings with her. She squished herself all the way on the floor of the car and covered herself carefully with the blanket. The seats on the back now looked empty and it seemed like only Suzi was in the car.

After a few minutes' drive, they entered the village and were passing road signs written in the Serbian cyrillic alphabet. It was hard to believe that they were only 10 kilometres away from Prishtina's city centre. It felt like a completely different country.

Ariana's heart pounded in her chest as she whispered from the floor of the car, her voice barely audible over the sound of the engine. "Do you know where you are going? Do you know the place?" she asked Suzi, her eyes darting nervously around the cramped space.

"Yes, of course I do," she told her, her eyes fixed firmly on the road ahead. As they drove deeper into the night, a gnawing fear began to take hold of Ariana. It occurred to her that she had told no one of their destination, leaving herself at the mercy of Suzi and her Serbian friends. What if they decided to kill her, to toss her body into some remote ditch and leave her to rot? No one would ever know what had become of her.

"Slow down!" she asked Suzi, her hands shaking as she reached for her phone inside her shoulder bag that was still on her shoulder. With deft fingers, she began to type out a message to Bashkim and continued to talk to Suzi.

"Remember, I have nothing to lose if you tell them to kill me," she told Suzi, her voice low and urgent. "But think about yourself and your children. If you do this, you'll have to deal with those people forever. They're criminals, Suzi. You'll lose everything - your freedom, your children, your reputation. Is that what you really want?" "Only I can save you at this moment" Ariana told her.

Suzi's voice was choked with emotion as she responded, her loyalty to their friendship never in question. "I would never, ever let them kill you," she said, her eyes welling up with tears. "And I would never betray our friendship, unlike you. And I'm sure you know that."

"Bashkim now knows where we are," Ariana told Suzi, her voice trembling. "He'll alert the police if I go missing."

"If you go missing then I'll go missing too" Suzi said.

"We're in this together," she told her, as strange as that sounded.

Ariana believed her. She covered herself completely with the blanket and tried to stay focused. She was nervous with fear, with anticipation of meeting the guy that had brutally ended her life even if he didn't kill her. He had let her live to suffer, to live with the memory of the tragedy every day for the rest of her life.

The car jolted and bumped along the rough, dark roads that

wound through the tiny village, jarring Ariana's nerves and making her grip the gun even tighter, under the blanket. Suddenly, Suzi's urgent voice pierced the silence. "Cover your head! Now!!" she hissed, her tone urgent and panicked.

Heart pounding in her chest, Ariana pulled the blanket over her head, huddling low in the floor of the car as Suzi deftly turned the car and came to a stop. Outside, a dog barked; Ariana heard the sound of footsteps approaching the car, her hands shaking as she clutched the gun close to her chest.

Suzi rolled down the window and spoke in rapid Serbian, her voice cool and collected despite the tension that hung heavy in the air. "Good evening," she said, her words barely audible to Ariana because of her rapid breathing. "Tell Zoran, Suzana is here."

"There's no way I will get out of here alive," Ariana thought, her fear mounting with each passing moment. Outside, she could hear the angry voices of men shouting and swearing.

Suzana was now telling someone that she wouldn't get out of the car and if they wanted to talk to her, they would have to come to the car.

Ariana braced herself as she heard the passenger door opening, her grip on the gun tighter with each passing moment. She tried to steady her breath, but she was afraid that her body would betray her. The man's voice, rough and guttural, dredged up memories she had tried so hard to bury and she would have liked to keep them buried forever. She could feel the goosebumps forming on her skin and her heart racing as the man's words filled the car.

All the years spent trying to forget the worst parts of that day and this man's presence had brought everything flooding back. His hoarse voice, his snickering laugh, and the profanity-laced sentences were etched in her mind, as if carved with a knife.

Ariana lay trembling on the floor of the car, anger boiling within her, her hand tightly gripping the gun. Her mind raced with thoughts of revenge, but she knew she had to wait, to bide her time. "Not yet, not yet... wait, wait," she said to herself.

Ariana was still trembling with fear as she listened to the heated exchange between Suzi and the man. The tension in the air was palpable, and she could sense the danger lurking in the darkness. Suzi's angry voice pierced the night, accusing the man of putting her in grave danger. As the argument escalated, the man's voice grew louder, drowning out Suzi's cries. His words were sharp and commanding, leaving no room for argument. Ariana strained to catch every word, her finger hovering over the trigger of her gun. Suddenly, the man bellowed, "Quiet!" and Ariana flinched at the force of his command. The sound echoed through the car, silencing Suzi.

She knew that things had just taken a dangerous turn. Ariana's body twitched so hard that she thought she would get discovered.. but the man, reeking of alcohol, seemed to be too drunk to notice anything.

"This was an emergency and we had to take this risk. There was no other way" he screamed. He then lowered his voice and he said to Suzi:

"After this you can quit, nothing will ever be required of you. Plus...pluuusssss,

he said not letting Suzi talk after she started to say something, "You will get full access to your brother who is alive but not so well in this hospital in Belgrade." he told her, passing her a piece of paper. Suzi gasped "All these years you kept me away knowing very well that I could see him?" Suzi shouted.

The words of the man made Ariana's blood boil, and she felt a sickening feeling in her stomach. How could they use Suzi's brother as leverage to manipulate her into doing their dirty work? She could hear Suzi's heart-wrenching sobs, as the man callously dangled her brother's fate in front of her. "My brother is alive, and you never told me till now?" Suzi asked again, crying.

Ariana couldn't fathom the depths of depravity of these people. She clenched her fists. "No need to cry, " the man was telling her. " What we're asking of you is a small little job. This will be easy, peasy and then you are free. You should be happy."

Ariana listened carefully as she waited for Suzi's response. She prayed that Suzi would not give in to their demands, that she would not put herself or anyone else in danger. But she also knew that the situation was not that simple. Suzi had already been caught up in their web of lies and deceit, and it would not be easy for her to break free.

Suzi's voice was shaking as she spoke, and Ariana could hear the fear and desperation in her tone. She had never heard Suzi like this before. "I won't do anything if you don't let my brother go free first!" she demanded. "I want to see him first. I want to make sure that he is alive and safe as I don't trust your words. I don't trust anything that you're saying" she hissed! "I want you to guarantee an escape from this country for me, my brother and my children" Suzi said sniffling and sounding very upset. "I want passports, money and everything for us to be able to escape."

The man's drunken laughter only added to the tension in the car. Ariana gripped the gun even tighter, her knuckles turning white.

Hehehehe.......the drunken man laughed sarcastically.

"Oooo....So you can tell that what we're asking of you is THAT important that we can't say no to any of your demands huh?" His sarcastic tone made it clear that he had no intention of fulfilling her request. "How do you know what I will be asking of you eh?"

"You better tell me if the Albanian bastards already know what we're planning to do" "Do they?" He shouted again.

"No," said Suzi "I don't know anything. I'm assuming that it's something big if it requires this kind of meeting right here, so close to Prishtina. I have no intention of putting my children's lives and mine at risk neither for the Albanians nor for Serbs. Not for you or anyone" Suzi was saying. "But you lied to me all this time about the fate of my brother so I need proof and commitment before I agree to anything."

There was a rapid movement and Ariana heard Suzi's laboured breathing and her difficulty in trying to say something. The man put his hands around Suzi's throat and was squeezing her neck hard. "You know I can kill you right here, right now" he hissed at Suzi.

"Not yet, Not yet!" Ariana was telling herself while her knuckles were hurting from clenching the gun. "Sweetheart, you know I'm a gentleman and you don't want to make me leave you to discuss these things with my friends out there." He said in a drunken snickering voice again at Suzi and then released her throat. Suzi was gasping for air but she wouldn't budge. "Go ahead!" she told him in a hush voice and started hitting him. "My husband will find you at the end of the world and kill you. Without me you will never have access to the information that you want. I bet your superiors won't be happy about that!"

"Call the hospital right now!" She was adamant. "I want to talk to my brother"

The drunken man seemed to be relenting. He opened his phone and dialled a number. He was talking to someone for a few minutes and then handed the phone to Suzi. "Hello, hello" said Suzi in a meek voice. "Alex is this you?" she asked him in Serbian "It's Suzi! Your sister Suzi" she said. "Are you Ok?" she asked him in Albanian now. "Please don't cry" she was telling him in Albanian "just listen to me!" "I will come and get you as soon as I can. I'll come tomorrow" she told him. "I've got the address, I know where you are! I'll come and get you tomorrow and we'll be together, don't you worry!" Suzi was trying to keep her voice steady. She sounded relieved, happy and sad at the same time. She was shaken. She said goodbye to her brother and handed the phone to the man.

"After you finish your mission successfully, we will talk again about the arrangement. But now you have to listen to me very carefully" he told her.

"The US special envoy for the Balkans is set to arrive in Prishtina on Monday, with the US ambassador hosting an exclusive dinner in his honour", he said. Among the carefully selected guests, your husband Bashkim and all the other key members of the government, accompanied by their spouses, are expected to be there.

Suzi's heart sank upon hearing the man's words.

"You will have to be there with your husband," he commanded.

Suzi interrupted him in a panic, "Wait, wait...don't you know that me and my husband are separated? He won't take me to that dinner."

But the man had anticipated her dilemma.

"That's why I invited you here personally," he said with a sly smile.

"You will go to his office on Monday, meet with your husband and convince him to take you with him. You use any method you like to convince him, but you will have to be there at that dinner."

"Why?" Suzi was saying, her voice trembling "I'm sure any important thing would be discussed in meetings, not during a dinner party. I won't find out anything during dinner. It will all be pointless chit chat."

"We don't need you to find out anything" the man was raising his voice and was obviously annoyed with Suzi now

"Can you shut the f... up for a few minutes and let me give you directions?"

"You will take this" he told Suzi "and put it in his drink. Do you understand?"

There was silence...

Ariana stopped herself from gasping.

"What?" Suzi shouted with surprise and fear in her voice.

"You want me to poison the US envoy? What the hell is wrong with you? I can't do that! I'm a mother. What will happen to my children if I get caught?. And I will get caught."

She started sobbing again.

"Yes you can! The man told her. And you will! Otherwise you will never see your children again! Ever!"

"No one will suspect you, we already have a story that the press will put out. We have a perfect person who will be blamed for it, a devout Muslim, working in the embassy's kitchen will be blamed. Do not mess this up, or you will regret it dearly!"

"Please no" "Suzi was pleading with him now "I can't do that, I'm not a killer, I can't do that!!!.."

"Yes, you can!" The man was telling Suzi and he lit up a cigarette.

"It's very simple and straightforward." And you are the only one who can do this.

He was inhaling his cigarette deeply and then he opened the window and shouted at the guys outside:

"Hey guys, go inside and wait there. I need a little privacy with my princess here hehehe" he said loudly snickering.

"Of course, boss" a voice from outside said and laughs were heard while the men outside were moving away.

"Hey princess" stop crying" "Come let me cheer you up"

All the rage that Ariana had felt for years came at a boiling point at that moment when she knew what he was trying to do. The man was trying to lift Suzi's dress with one hand and pull her towards himself, as she was pushing him away and started slapping his face.

"You disgusting pig!" She was saying in half breaths while hitting him.

"It's time" Ariana told herself and pushed the blanket aside and jumped quickly from the car floor. With a sudden burst of courage, Ariana emerged from the back seat of the car and swiftly pressed her hand firmly over his mouth and the gun to his temple. "Don't you move, you bastard!" she spat in Serbian, feeling defiled for having to touch him. . The man was so taken aback by her sudden attack that he froze in terror, much to the shock of Suzi who was hitting him furiously. "You fool! You worthless piece of...!" she shouted in a rage.

Ariana, still holding the gun to the man's head, commanded Suzi to take his weapon. As Suzi followed her orders and pointed the second gun at him, the three of them were locked in a tense standoff.

"start driving and keep the lights off," Ariana told Suzi.

She was squeezing the man's mouth with all her force!

All the skills that she learned in the Police Academy were coming to use.

"Make a sound and you're dead!" she told him

Suzi was reversing the car with the lights off.

"Drive! Drive!" Ariana told her

The man grabbed Ariana's hand and tried to release himself from her grasp.

She moved the gun and pointed it on his crotch.

He was breathing heavily now and was trying to say something and was looking sideways at Suzi with wide open eyes, in shock.

Ariana twisted his neck forcefully and told him

"You might not remember me but you made a great mistake for letting me live that cold morning of 1999. You killed the love of my life and took advantage of an innocent child like me. You f... coward!!!! You let me live and suffer. Well,here I am in the name of all the victims taking revenge, you son of a b....!"

She pulled the trigger and hit him on his crotch. Suzi let out a scream and stopped the car.

"Ariana NO...she told her. Don't do it..he's not worth it.."

Ariana pulled the trigger one more time. This time on his right leg.

Another muffled scream as Ariana was still holding his mouth.

She quickly leaned over and opened the car door and pushed him out of the car with force.

She Closed the door and said to Suzi:

"Drive! Drive!!" She turned back and looked at the man left in the side of the street wailing loudly. And she felt a mixture of guilt, relief, happiness, sadness, all in one. The rush of adrenaline made her body shiver. Her tears flew down her face as she smiled and sobbed at the same time. Ariana's laughter was uncontrollable as Suzana sped down the highway, leaving their tormentor far behind.

"Wooohooo!" Ariana exclaimed, as if struck by a temporary madness. "I did it! I hope he survives and suffers for the rest of his life like I am!"

As Suzana weaved through traffic, she looked pale and more scared. "Oh my god, Oh my god," she muttered, shaking. "What now? What do we do now?"

Ariana took a deep breath and looked at her phone. It was only 9 pm.

"Now we go back to the party" Ariana said "The party is not over yet!"

Her text message to Bashkim was never delivered.

"Try again!" Her phone was suggesting. She deleted it!

"Are you sure?" Suzi was saying "Those men will come after us"

"No they won't" said Ariana as she was calling the police.

Once they were on the highway next to the Albi mall, full of lights and traffic and cheerful people going shopping or meeting with friends, they both started to feel safer.

"Allo" said Ariana on the phone "There's some shooting being reported in Graçanicë, second street on the left from the monastery, fifth house. There are Serbian nationals that entered the country illegally. I'm a KS interior ministry staff member and I will report this to the Minister right away. You get on your way immediately!!"

With that, she hung up the phone and leaned back into the car seat, feeling a sense of relief that she had taken action. Suzana glanced over at her, her eyes wide with worry.

"What did you do?" she asked, her voice trembling.

"I reported it to the authorities," Ariana replied calmly. "We can't just sit by and let these things happen. We have to do something."

Suzana nodded in agreement, her hands gripping the steering wheel tightly as they continued down the highway. The city lights blurred outside, a sharp contrast to the tension and danger they had just left behind.

Ariana turned to Suzana, her eyes filled with gratitude. "Thank you for not betraying me! And thank you for giving me this opportunity to take my revenge!" she said, her voice filled with emotion. Suzi looked at her, her own eyes shining with tears. "What will happen now?" she asked, her voice trembling slightly.

"You will destroy that old phone that you have. We will tell Bashkim everything, and then we will decide how to protect you and your children from possible retaliation," Ariana said, her tone reassuring. "You have to go and get your brother out of that hospital as soon as possible" "And..." she continued "you will have to tell us everything, from the beginning," she added, her expression serious. She felt sorry now for Suzi, understanding what she had been going through all this time. "Don't worry! Everything will be fine!" she told her and reached to tap her in the shoulder. "I will try and protect you from any infraction with the law as I know and believe you were a victim of blackmail". " But now, let's go and finish those drinks at the party," Ariana said, her smile returning.

The police sirens were wailing loudly as they passed by, heading in the opposite direction.

"We're crazy!" Suzi said, with a hint of fear in her voice.

"We're awesome!" Ariana replied, grinning.

"We look terrible," Suzi said, glancing at herself in the car mirror as they pulled into a parking space near the banquet hall.

"We look like warriors!" Ariana said, pulling out a comb and some powder and makeup from her bag and handing them to Suzi.

As Ariana and Suzana stepped out of the car, Ariana quickly covered the front seat with her blanket and left the windows slightly open. Despite the gruesome scene, Ariana felt a sense of liberation. She will remember this night for as long as she lives. She hoped the past horrors in her mind would fade and be replaced with the knowledge that she got revenge, no matter if she might regret everything tomorrow. The world seemed more just than it was a couple of hours ago. She clenched her fists and muttered "I hope he suffers a lot," then she straightened her dress and fixed her hair, determined to present a composed and collected facade as if nothing had happened. There was a bitter feeling deep in her gut, and she was a little surprised when she felt it. "I'm not going to feel bad for that criminal!" she told herself. "He had no mercy for me, a 19-year-old innocent, helpless girl, so there's no way I'm letting myself feel guilty for what I did to him." She pushed aside the bitterness and the twinge of sadness, realising that revenge wasn't going to make her forget her horrors after all. It might only make her realise that everyone is capable of doing terrible things to a fellow human and that the world and humanity were deeply flawed.

As they re-joined the party , the music seemed more melodious to Ariana's ears, and she started to engage with people. She now interacted with them differently; she was able to look into their eyes, nodding and smiling warmly. Ariana even took the time to greet Arben's friends, who hugged her and expressed their condolences about Arben and her family. Unlike earlier in the evening, she managed to smile and laugh at their jokes, and listened with enjoyment to their anecdotes of mischief with Arben from high school. It was as if a heavy weight had been lifted from her shoulders.

Suzana scurried towards the bar, her hands still trembling with anxiety as she ordered herself another cocktail. The last one had been left untouched, but now she needed more alcohol to boost her courage in order to confront Bashkim. She wanted to have one more drink before calling a taxi to take her home. She didn't think she could endure staying at the party any longer.

She sipped her drink and her mind was preoccupied with the scenarios of how Bashkim will react to all that happened tonight. Would he understand that she had to do whatever it took to protect their children or would he find what she did unforgivable? What will the law's repercussions be? Will he help her to go and get her brother from that hospital? She couldn't believe she had finally found Alex. The thought of reuniting with her brother filled her with hope, making her believe that things might finally turn for the better. She envisioned their reunion, imagining the joy and relief of having a part of her lost family back. With Alex by her side, she might feel grounded and protected, a sense of belonging she hadn't felt in years.

With a deep breath, Suzana took her cocktail and returned to the table, settling into her chair and trying to maintain a calm exterior. She didn't feel like going home yet; the distraction from what was coming and the ability to postpone whatever was about to happen suited her just fine. No one at the party had noticed her absence, and she intended to keep it that way. She could deny any accusations of being involved in the shooting in Graçanicë. A wave of relief washed over her at the thought. "Ariana is a genius," she mused. Maybe Ariana would never tell Bashkim about any of this. The police would only deal with the armed criminals who had entered the country illegally, leaving her completely out of it.

She saw Besa coming over to sit down at the table and moved to sit next to her. The heat of the dance floor had clearly taken its toll on Besa, and she was desperately trying to cool down. Besa smiled at her as she huffed and puffed while sitting down.

"Hey," Besa said "Where have you guys been? I kept looking and couldn't see you anywhere."

Suzi responded with a sheepish grin. "Me and Ariana were outside smoking and talking. We got carried away."

What about Fatime? Where did she go?" Besa asked, looking around the hall.

"I think I saw Fatime sitting at a table next to the bar with some of her friends from the Science Club." Suzi answered.

Besa's face showed a brief moment of doubt.. "Oh," she said. "I started to get worried. I thought you guys abandoned me."

Suzi's smile grew wider. "Never!" she exclaimed, reaching out to give Besa's hand a reassuring squeeze. As she settled more comfortably into the seat next to Besa, Suzi thought of an exciting idea.

"Tell me about America," she asked Besa eagerly, her thoughts already drifting towards the possibility of moving to the land of the free.

"I want to take my kids to Disney World in Florida." she said, feeling invigorated by the thought. Besa could send her a formal invitation letter that she could use to obtain a visa.

"Oh, I wouldn't know where to start," Besa said.

"America is whatever one makes of it, I guess. It gives you a feeling that anything is possible and you actually feel that kind of freedom there. You start to believe it offers unlimited possibilities as well as the freedom to be who you are or want to be. Yet like everywhere else, there are so many downsides too."

Suzi nodded thoughtfully, her mind already working on the logistics of a trip to the States. "Yes, I can imagine," she said. "But it sounds like a great place to me!"

"I think I will get tickets as soon as I can," Suzi continued. "I've been thinking about visiting the US for a long time now, and I think now is the best time." Suzi recognized that her only chance to escape the Serbian Secret Service's grasp and embark on a fresh journey toward genuine freedom lay in relocating to the US. The two friends continued talking, their minds filled with visions of what could be. And for Suzi, the dream of America began to take on a new, more urgent meaning, as she contemplated the risks and rewards of leaving everything she had ever known behind.

"Does obtaining a US visa require some form of guarantee?" she asked Besa.

"I've heard that a visa can't be obtained without someone providing a guarantee. Could you perhaps draft an invitation letter for me and my children?"

She refrained from mentioning her brother to Besa at the moment but she thought about how she would bring him along.

"I don't think you need anything, especially if you're going as a tourist," Besa said, her voice soft and soothing. " I'd be happy to write a letter of recommendation for you. I will start working at the US embassy here in Prishtina this coming week" Besa said "As soon as I get settled I'll start looking at what I can do and what the procedure is. I'm sure you won't need my help at all. So many people travel to the US from Kosova nowadays that obtaining a visa shouldn't be a problem."

Suzi felt a weight lift off her shoulders, the prospect of a new life in America suddenly feeling within reach. "Thank you so much," she said, feeling truly grateful. "My kids will be so happy when I tell them." Suzi felt a glimmer of hope for the first time since this morning. The sense of gloom that she had felt all day and the loss of all hope after the events of a couple of hours ago in Graçanicë began to lift away from her mind. With Besa's help and advice, she knew that she could make a new life for herself, her children and her brother, one filled with the promise of unlimited possibilities and freedom. "Rron will have a chance to get a more thorough treatment and a normal life" she thought.

As the night wore on, all the ladies made their way to their seats at the table. Ariana and Fatime eventually arrived, their faces flushed from talking and laughing. The music had shifted to a slower tempo, and couples swayed together on the dance floor.

Fatime looked down at her watch, her expression one of surprise. "Ladies, can you believe it? It's almost midnight," she said, her voice filled with wonder. "Time flew by so quickly!"

Suzi couldn't believe how fast the night had passed, and she found herself wishing that it could go on forever. For a few brief moments, she had been able to forget about the danger that may be laying in wait for her. She was also dreading the plan to go to Belgrade for her brother. What can she do? Who could she send to get her brother out of the hospital? She would have to ask Bashkim to help her with that.

Fatime found herself amazed by the amount of energy she still possessed. At home, she would have been in bed for hours by now. She couldn't remember the last time that she stayed up this late but tonight here she was, caught up in the excitement of the moment and feeling energised and alive. Despite the joy she felt at being surrounded by her friends and dancing the night away, she couldn't shake the restlessness that lingered just beneath the surface. The fear and uncertainty that had been simmering inside her began to boil over. The what-ifs and worst-case scenarios raced through her mind like a series of crashing waves, threatening to overwhelm her. Desperate to finally feel free from her fears and insecurities, Fatime was thinking about her plan very seriously now. As the night wore on, her anxiety began to build until she could no longer contain it.

"I'm running away" she blurted out, her voice ringing out in the sudden silence at the table. The women looked at her, their expressions unreadable as they processed her words.

"I'm running away from my marriage and from the country!" Fatime repeated, her voice growing stronger with each word. As the gravity of what she was saying sank in she felt as though a burden had been lifted from her soul.

"Is that why you need the gun?" Ariana asked her calmly.

A hush fell over the table.

"How do you know about the gun,? Asked Fatime, puzzled, reaching under the table for her duffle bag.

"Be careful! It's still hot," Ariana warned, pulling out the gun slowly from her bag and wrapping it with a table napkin to conceal it from view.

"I shot the man who abused me during the war with it a couple of hours ago," Ariana said, handing the gun cautiously under the table to Fatime.

The women were stunned, trying to process the information. Besa, in particular, struggled to take in what she was hearing. Her eyes widened in shock, and she leaned in, doubting her ears. Suzi twirled her cocktail, her eyes misting up.

Besa struggled to understand what was going on; "What?" she exclaimed, before lowering her voice to a whisper. "I don't understand anything you ladies are talking about. What happened tonight?"

Suzi leaned over and filled her in, her voice low and urgent. "Me and Ariana weren't just standing outside, in fact we just came back from Graçanicë, and let me tell you, it was a crazy night." Suzi felt relieved to be talking about what happened. She turned her eyes towards Ariana and said "Our brave friend Ariana, who suffered all these years, keeping her abuse during the war a secret even from me, has finally got some justice for herself tonight."

Ariana's eyes welled up with tears as she reflected on the events of the past few hours, grateful for the dim lighting that veiled her emotions. As the soft strains of music floated in the background, a heavy silence enveloped the women, each lost in her own thoughts. The weight of the moment made conversation impossible.

Besa's face betrayed her sorrow and bewilderment. She couldn't comprehend why Ariana had kept this burden to herself for so long. Tears glistened in her eyes as she finally spoke, her voice barely above a whisper. "Oh God," she murmured, her gaze fixed on Ariana. "You carried this alone all these years? I can't begin to express how sorry I am."

Ariana wiped away her tears, the flood of emotions overwhelming her. Meanwhile, Fatime felt a pang of guilt for sharing her own troubles. At that moment, they seemed trivial compared to Ariana's pain. She closed her eyes briefly, offering a silent prayer for her friend.

Besa takes charge of the situation, determined to unravel the web of secrets and encourage her friends to open up to one another so they could share their thoughts and their pain just like when they were young, in her room.

"Let's start from the beginning," she said calmly, leaning forward and squeezing each of her friends' hands in turn and taking a deep breath.

The night stretched on like an endless sea, the four friends riding the waves of emotion. Their stories wove together, each thread connecting to the next in a tapestry of shared and separate experience. They talked of love and loss, of heartbreak and hope, of dreams that had been shattered and dreams that would yet have to be realised.

As the hours passed, the world around them grew still, the last of the patrons trickling out of the hall until they were alone in the semidarkness. The only sound was the soft murmur of their voices and the occasional clink of glasses as they shared another round of drinks.

As the night went on, their conversation showed no signs of slowing. It was as if they had been holding back for so long, and now that the dam had been breached, they couldn't stop the flood pouring forth.

The hall manager had long since given up on ushering them out, content to let them stay as long as they liked. And so they sat, the four of them, lost in each other's stories until the first light of dawn crept through the windows. The words flowed like a gentle stream, back and forth, back and forth, punctuated by laughter and tears that mingled in a symphony of emotions. Their bond grew stronger that night, cemented with unbreakable ties of friendship and the feeling that they were there for each other no matter what. Besa, the heart of the group, raised her glass, "To us!" she said "To our friendship and to our future! We shared the past but now we stop and look forward into our lives! Let us all have a healthy and happy rest of our lives." In response, her friends raised their own glasses, their faces alight with smiles that could light up the darkest of nights. The word "Gëzuar!" echoed through the room, a simple yet powerful expression of their determination to leave the past behind.

They laughed and cried and toasted to the night, to their friendship, and to the promise of tomorrow, each one grateful for the gift of each other's presence and they still couldn't call it a night. They decided to wait till the time came for Fatime's bus and her journey to Sarande.

"What is your idea of perfect happiness?" Besa asked suddenly , looking at all of them. It was a question from the Proust Questionnaire in The Vanity Fair Magazine that she loved to read. She always wanted to ask people that question.

Her question hung in the air like the sweet scent of flowers on a summer evening, each one of the four women lost in thought as they thought about the nature of true contentment. They got to think about happiness and the future for a moment and that was a novel idea, one that had rarely crossed their minds since their childhood. Even then, they had been conditioned to believe that happiness was something that could only be found through self-sacrifice, that to pursue it openly was seen as selfish and indulgent. In their culture, the concept of "unity" reigned supreme, with the happiness of the family and community always taking precedence over the individual. And usually it meant women were left last in line for care, support and finding fulfilment in life. World around them was hostile to the idea of their independence and individuality.

For a moment, they all sat in silence, their minds reeling with the implications of Besa's question.

Was it possible that their happiness, too, deserved to be considered and pursued?

Besa's words seemed like a call to action, a reminder that they were the masters of their own destinies. Those words sounded like a challenge that threatened to unsettle the very foundations of their beliefs. It became clear that not everyone was willing to accept her call to action. Ariana, in particular, seemed to take issue with Besa's assertion that they were the masters of their own destinies. "Ha..." muttered Ariana cynically. "Here comes Besa's indoctrination with the US ideology of the pursuit of happiness only possible by ignoring the reality" she laughed cynically.

To Ariana, the idea of being "a master of one's own destiny" was nothing but a cruel joke, a reminder of the war that had stolen their youth and left them adrift in a sea of uncertainty and they couldn't have done nothing about that, no matter how much they might have tried. For how could they be the masters of their own destinies when their lives had been shaped by circumstances beyond their control?

Through no fault of their own, their young lives and dreams and hopes were stolen from them forever, never to be returned. So how were they "masters" of their destinies?

Besa pretended to not have heard Ariana, her voice soft and gentle as she spoke of the joy she felt in that moment, surrounded by them, her dear friends that she loved most. Her words were a balm to their weary souls, a reminder of the simple pleasures that could bring the greatest happiness even after so much hardship and tragedy. "Life must go on" Besa said

The women raised their glasses in agreement, their faces alight with a sense of warmth and belonging. For in that moment, they knew that they were truly blessed to have met each other again.

And then Fatime spoke, her voice tinged with a sense of longing and hope. She spoke of her dream to live by the sea, of the freedom it would give her, of the way she hoped it would give her the much needed perspective on everything that she endured in life. She was in awe of her own words that described her long awaited dreams and were illuminating the imagination of a path to a future filled with possibility.

The girls cheered her on, their voices filled with love and support. They knew that her dream was within reach, that she was destined for greatness, and that they would be there every step of the way to support her in her journey.

"My perfect idea of happiness is being able to visit the graves of Arben and of my parents and siblings" Ariana said finally. "I would be relieved if I ever get to put them in their final place of rest. That I think will be the only way for me to be able to get peace and move on with my life."

Her words touched them all deeply and they all stood up to hug her in silence. The war had stolen their innocence, their youth, and their loved ones. It had left them with wounds that would never truly heal. "The crimes committed by Milosevic's rabid nationalists are too great to be forgotten, too grave to be ignored". The anger and frustration in Ariana's voice reverberated around the hall. They all knew that there was no easy solution to the pain and suffering they had endured. But for this moment, at least, they found comfort in each other's presence and in the hope that somehow, they might find a way to move forward. That night they let the past, present, and future be intertwined, a tapestry of joy and sorrow, hope and despair.

"The way I spent my childhood, is my perfect idea of happiness," Suzi said, her voice a soft echo of childhood memories. Beneath her nostalgia lay a deep sadness, a yearning for a time long gone. The present held no comparison to the bliss of her childhood, and the weight of reality pressed heavily upon her heart every day. Suzi sighed, knowing that the world she had been yearning for could never return, forever altered by the war that had ravaged it.

Besa, however, refused to give in to despair.

"I think we can overcome or at least try our best to overcome the tragedies that have happened to us. We must! And that's what we're doing" she said. Though the tragedies they had faced had changed them irrevocably, she believed that they could still strive for a brighter future. With unshakable optimism, she spoke of their resilience, of their determination to overcome the hardships they had endured.

"It's so hard." Fatime siad. Fatime's voice was tinged with bitterness, a reflection of the harshness of their reality. She spoke of the cruelty that surrounded them, of the chains of traditions and expectations that held sway over their lives. For her, the task of overcoming their trials was a daunting one, exacerbated by the hostility they faced as women in society, some parts of which instead of moving forward, were going back deeper into patriarchy.

"True," Besa agreed. Her voice was heavy with weariness born of experience of hardships as a woman in the West too.

"How's life with James?" Asked Suzi trying to change the subject.

"Ooo I dream of just once in my lifetime making love to an American" she said out loud, looking up at the ceiling holding her hands as if in a prayer. The women roared with laughter.

Her words were both startling and amusing, and the women erupted into much needed peals of laughter, momentarily forgetting their worries.

"As our relationship soured, I drifted away. It's not my fault maybe that i didn't know how to handle this feeling as if I had been plucked out of my world and cast away in a foreign land" she said. It took her a long time in that displacement, to find a newfound sense of independence, a strength that she had not known existed within her.

Though the divorce from James had been painful, she had discovered that the greatest love was the love of oneself. "If you don't love yourself, ultimately no one can." Besa said. "If you're not kind to yourself or try to heal yourself from whatever you need healing from, no one can and to come to that awareness or enlightenment if you will, it took time because I didn't have a parent, a friend or a mentor to teach me these things. I had to figure it out myself."

Despite the pain that lingered, she could look back on their time together with a measure of acceptance, secure in the knowledge that she had grown stronger for having known him.

"He is a nice guy. We're good friends" Besa finally said.

"Oh how I wish Agim would be friends with me again" sighed Fatime, her voice tinged with a longing for a past that she knew could never be regained. As she spoke of Agim, her eyes filled with tears, and her voice trembled with emotion.

"I tried to reach out to him, to bridge the gap that had formed between us, but he had retreated into himself, and the walls of his pain had become impenetrable" Fatime said. She was left with a sense of loss, of a love that had withered away, despite her best efforts to hold onto it.

Suzi wrapped her arms around Fatime, offering her the comfort of a friend's embrace. "It's not your fault," she whispered into her friend's ear. Such abandonment, Suzi said, was something some people could inflict upon their partners when they were battling within themselves.

Even Ariana, who was now with Suzi's unfaithful husband, seemed to understand the cruel nature of love. Her gaze fell to the ground as Suzi spoke of Bashkim's infidelities. Sensing Ariana's unease, Suzi reached out and took her hand. "I'm not mad at you," she said, her voice gentle. "I'm actually glad that he's with someone I know and trust. My children will have a wonderful stepmother whenever they visit their dad." Ariana opened her mouth to speak, but Suzi cut her off, her voice rising in encouragement. "I hope you marry him. Don't be stubborn," she urged. "Life should go on, and you deserve to be happy."

Ariana reached for her wine glass and raised it. The clinking of glasses resonated through the room, a sweet melody of friendship. She raised her wine glass high, inviting her friends to join her in a toast. "Cheers to the living!" she exclaimed, "Cheers to wonderful friends! Cheers to us!" Her words hung in the air like a warm embrace. As they raised their glasses and clicked them together, the memories of their childhood flooded back. They were transported to a simpler time, where their only worry was how to best spend their recess and summer vacations. Harsh reality had soon caught up with them, and the horrors of war had separated them. Suffering, and loss had come knocking at their doors, and they didn't have the option of keeping it shut. . Despite all that, their friendship had endured, a shining beacon of hope and resilience. In that moment, they wished for a way to turn back time, to undo the pain and trauma that had befallen them.

———

When they finally told each other everything and they had given each other one last hug, they all made their way towards the door to leave.

They opened the heavy entrance door of the venue and the sun came rushing in, immersing their silhouettes in a warm yellow glow. It was already a beautiful morning outside. The warmth of the sun enveloped them in a comforting embrace. The sky above was painted in shades of blue, with fluffy white clouds floating serenely. The early morning in the city was beautiful and today even the sky above appeared to radiate with a glow of hope. The air was crisp and fresh, free from the heavy burden of war and oppression that had once hovered like a low cloud.

The women made their way across the street, towards a coffee shop on the terrace of the old Youth Center . Memories of concerts and parties hosted at the venue before the war, flooded their minds as they walked, their high heels clacking against the pavement.

"Do you remember when we came to the concerts and parties that were held here?

I don't think we missed any of them!" Said Besa, smiling.

"Oh, I remember all of them," Suzi said smiling.

Despite their makeup being smudged and hair being messily tied, they wore smiles on their faces, radiating the joy of the night they had just spent together. At the coffee shop, they ordered cups of warm coffee and sweet treats and they savoured the last few moments before Fatime's departure for Sarande. The city was already full of people rushing to go to work. Some of them were stopping to have their morning coffee before heading to their offices.

The hustle and bustle of people going about their daily routines was a sight to behold. The aroma of freshly brewed coffee wafted through the air, blending with the sweet scent of blooming flowers. The girls noticed lots of buses full of young women, getting off the bus in front of the centre and going to the city stadium. They saw a swarm of women eagerly gathering around the entrance of the stadium. "There must be something going on at the city stadium," said Ariana.

"Oh I know what's going on" Suzi said "It is an exhibition by a conceptual artist. I was invited to it, in fact. It is supposed to be very interesting. Why don't we go and see what's happening". After they finished their coffees, they stood up and started joining the crowds of women heading towards the stadium. Upon entering, they paused, perplexed by the sight before them.

Throughout the vast expanse of the arena, rows upon rows of clotheslines hung, upon which groups of young women were carefully draping dresses, skirts, and pants. It looked as though the entire nation had chosen the city's stadium as a place to dry their laundry that day. The kaleidoscope of colours and patterns, like an endless sea of strange flags, drew attention in a very unusual way! It was something you weren't really meant to look at but couldn't ignore. Through a brochure that was given to them they realised that the concept was that each garment, without a single word, written or said, would convey a poignant and painful narrative - a tale of silent suffering endured by countless victims of war and rape. For every item of clothing hanging before them, there was a story of a life shattered and a broken soul. A thousand sorrows that dared not speak their name, now laid bare before their eyes.

Softly, a gentle breeze fluttered the garments, as if to comfort them.. Above them, the banners hanging from the stadium's bleachers carried a message: "Thinking of You".

As Ariana knelt on the lush grass, she surrendered to the weight of her emotions, unable to contain the tears that streamed down her face. She buried her head in her hands, not shielding her grief from the world anymore.

Besa stood in awe, her eyes locked on the endless sea of vibrant colours that filled the stadium. It was as if each piece of clothing was a living being , mourning the loss and pain of the countless women who had suffered the horrors of war and sexual violence. Thousands of colourful fabrics seemed to be mourning the lives of the women of her generation. For a moment, time stood still, as the weight of the past and the present collided. A moment of collective mourning. The deafening silence that hung in the air was a constant reminder of the painful memories that had been etched into her body and soul. As she made her way through the rows of clotheslines, she moved slowly, aiming to give each garment due respect and attention. There were so many garments, each one telling a different story, each one holding a unique secret, each one bearing witness to the tremendous pain that had been inflicted on countless men and women. The simple garments, devoid of any sound or voice, stood as a powerful testament to the lost lives and shattered youth of those who had suffered in silence.

For a moment, it seemed as though everyone had finally come together to release their painful stories. The clothes, draped across the lines, stood as a visual representation of the wounds that could not be spoken, demanding to be seen, to be understood.

But could justice ever truly be served? Was there any remedy that could ease the weight of the pain that had been carried for so long? The scars would remain, the wounds would ache. And yet, in this moment, there was a glimmer of hope - a hope that perhaps by acknowledging the past, by recognizing the pain that had been inflicted, there was a chance to move forward towards a future.

Besa's footsteps slowed as she carefully approached a pink nightgown swaying on the third row of clotheslines. She reached out with trembling fingers, brushing the delicate fabric with a gentle touch. A faded photo of Sleeping Beauty adorned the front, and the princess looked back at her with a soft, knowing smile. As Besa gazed at the nightgown, tears blurred her vision and deep in her head she heard the ever present knocks on the door: boom, boom, boom.

THE END

ACKNOWLEDGMENTS

I'd like to express my deep respect and admiration to the women of Kosova that lived through the war, for their strength, resilience and sacrifices.

I hope this book, written from my heart, serves as a worthy tribute.

I thank my family and my dear friends for their support and encouragement.

Special thanks to my wonderful editors: Linda Baleta and Bekim Bërlajolli for their advice, vision and their skills.

I also wanted to extend my gratitude to the amazing artist Fitore Berisha for providing her beautiful painting for the cover of my book. The emotion captured in her work perfectly encapsulates the essence of my story, it elevates the visual appeal of my book and I am thrilled to share it with the world.

And lastly, thank you to The Paper House Publishing Company for their generous cooperation and help in making my dream come true.

ABOUT THE AUTHOR

ILIRIANA RAMA ALLAJBEGU was born in Kosovo in 1969. She studied English Language and Literature at the University of Prishtina till senior level when the University closed to Albanian students and staff. She moved to London, UK and graduated from London Metropolitan University in 1999. She lives in New Jersey with her family. The Reunion is her first novel.